Richard Carpenter's

ROBIN OF SHERWOOD

TO HAVE AND TO HOLD

by Elliot Thorpe

Originally published in 2020 by
Chinbeard Books & Spiteful Puppet
in partnership with the
Richard Carpenter Estate
The edition published in 2021
www.spitefulpuppet.com

Layout & adaptation for this edition by
Andrews UK Limited
www.andrewsuk.com

CONTENTS

PROLOGUE

The huge tithe barn adjacent to the main cloisters of St Mary's Abbey was overflowing with harvested grain. It was also beginning to smell.

'Their souls will go to Hell for this,' Abbott Hugo de Rainault sneered, staring at the rotting mounds. 'All this ruined because they can't keep a few seeds away from a couple of rats.'

'It's been a wet winter, my Lord Abbot,' declared Brother Gregory, his voice quavering. He knew full well the wrath his abbot could wield even at the slightest provocation. Stating the obvious was probably not a good idea.

'Don't you think I know that, idiot?'

'The vermin have taken shelter in the barn.'

'Why should they? They don't pay the Church any tithes.' Hugo yelled at Gregory. 'Get that grain moved and thrown away. Then send word to the peasants that they'll need to replace it all.'

Hugo tried to ignore the figure lurking nervously by the cloisters as Gregory scurried away.

'If I may, Abbot Hugo?' The new figure, finally plucked up the courage to approach.

'What is it?' Hugo spat. 'Ah, Andrew, isn't it? What brings you here to witness this rotting mass?'

Andrew, a veteran of the Crusades, surveyed the sense, but made no comment on it. 'I have new my Lord Abbot. News which will be of interest to both you and the Sheriff of Nottingham.

'What can possibly be more important than this disaster?' Hugo asked, waving his arms at the rotten grain.

'There is to be a wedding.'

'A wedding? I've given no such blessing.'

'It's to be held in Wickham.'

'The confounded arrogance of that damnable Edward.'

'I overheard one of my servants speaking. It is to involve one of Robin Hood's outlaws.' Andrew almost whispered the last word.

Hugo's eyes widened. 'It's not that Tuck imbecile, is it? Marrying off the peasants to each other?'

'No, my Lord Abbot. One of the outlaws themselves is to wed.'

Hugo shook his head in disgust. 'Who would deign to be married to a wolfshead? Do you know which one?'

CHAPTER 1

Little John sat amongst the trees that surrounded the edge of the lake. On warm barmy evenings he'd often sit at the water's edge; watching the mayflies as they tried to avoid the swifts and martins, which swooped from great heights to catch them. He'd listen to the warble of the nightjars and the rustling of the crickets. Sometimes he'd stay there until the sun disappeared behind the trees, its ochre glow dappled by the rippling water, to be replaced by the rising moon that bathed the lake and the treetops in a silvery, pearly glow.

He'd come here now, at the break of day, to avoid Will's teasing. He'd been doing his best to pretend it didn't annoy him, but his patience was being tested a little too sorely of late.

John's moment of peace, however, wasn't destined to last. The lake wasn't far from their current camp, and soon Will and Tuck had found him staring into the water.

'Thinking of ending it all? Going to throw yourself in?' Scarlet laughed. 'You only asked Meg to marry you because she's so short! She's so far away from you that I bet you didn't hear her reply properly—even with those big ears!'

Tuck breathed out through pursed lips. 'You're pushing your luck there, Will!'

'Who would bat an eyelid at a little marrying a Little?' crowed Will, thumping the sitting giant on his broad shoulders.

'Right, that's it, lad…you've asked for this…' John launched himself to his full height, grabbing his quarterstaff on the way up. 'Come here. I'll wipe that smile off your face!'

1

A grinning Will dashed into the trees and John gave chase, roaring hellfire into the air. Tuck chuckled and walked back to their encampment.

***

'He's not really angry is he, Tuck?' Much asked as the friar explained what had happened.

'Of course not.' Tuck's gentle voice calmed Much's anxiety. 'Listen…' He raised a chubby finger then nodded, returning his attention to the bubbling pot of stew over the campfire. 'You can hear then laughing together. John will probably throw Will into the lake and they'll come back soaked to the skin, shoulder to shoulder, all smiles. You'll see.'

'You boys will never grow up,' said Marion, her auburn hair glowing in the morning sunlight that was streaming through the trees.

'Good morning, Little Flower.'

Marion smiled as she sat next to the friar. 'It's chilly today.'

'This will warm you up.' Tuck handed her a bowl of hot stew.

'Thank you. Where's Robin?'

'He went out early,' said Much. 'Herne had something to tell him.'

Tuck saw Marion tense. Herne hadn't called on Robin in weeks, not since their unpleasant encounter with Morgwyn of Ravenscar. Something serious must have happened for Robin to have been summoned before sunrise.

'I'm sure everything will be fine.' Tuck gave Marion his bet reassuring smile.

Will and John came stumbling into the camp. Their faces were red with laughter, their body's soaked with pond water. Thumping themselves down near the fire, they helped themselves to Tuck's cooking.

Talk soon turned to John's impending nuptials and Will promised not to make any more fun of them. For now.

'Where will you live?' asked Marion.

'Are you leaving us, John?' Much moved to sit next to his tall friend. 'You're not, are you?'

Asking Meg to be his wife was the right thing for them both, but he knew that leaving the group wasn't possible. They'd tried to leave together before, and fate had soon bought John back to Sherwood again. He could never expect Meg to join them in Sherwood and he feared that a life in Wickham would make him unhappy, even if he were with the love of his life. Anyway, if a known outlaw were to live openly in Wickham, every villager there would be in danger from the sheriff. Edward and his people took enough risks for the outlaws anyway. So, they'd decided to make the best of the life they had; Meg in Wickham and John in Sherwood – meeting as often as they could.

John looked at his friends, before he turned back to Much's anxious face. 'Of course I'm not leaving. As if I would!'

***

Robin was tired.

Disturbed by dark dreams and the coldness of the night, he hadn't slept well. Now, as Robin returned from Herne's cave, he sat by the fire, taking Marion's hand and holding it tight as he shared what the Lord of the Trees had told him.

'Herne warned me that we'd be captured.'

'That's something that could happen anytime if we don't 'ave our wits about us,'

Will frowned into the fire.

'There must be something about this warning that's different though, for Herne to have called you away so early.' Marion pushed Robin's blonde locks away from his face.

'He told me of a maiden who would need rescuing from Nottingham castle. We'd all be captured in the process.'

'*All* of us? That doesn't make sense. Why would we be there?' John asked.

'Who is the maiden, Robin?' Marion held his gaze. 'Is it me?'

Robin nodded slowly. 'It has to be. Rescuing you from the castle is the only reason we'd all be there together.'

'Robin's right. There's no way any of us would stay behind if you'd been captured.' Will stood, arching his back, his clothes still wet from his tussle in the lake with John. 'So, one of us will need to stay with Marion at all times to make sure she doesn't get captured in the first place.'

'I don't need to be treated like a child!'

'No one would do that, Marion,' said Robin. 'We just need to make sure you aren't taken to the castle.'

'I suppose so.' Marion agreed, 'but don't go forgetting I'm as strong as any of you when it comes to defending myself and the people of Sherwood!'

Robin squeezed her hand, 'A fact you have proved to us a hundred times over.'

'Come with me to Wickham,' John piped up. 'You can help Meg prepare for the wedding.'

'That's a good idea, John,' Robin turned to Marion, 'You'll be safe in Wickham with Edward and the others. If the sheriff is planning to take you, for whatever reason, they won't imagine you'd be anywhere else except in Sherwood.'

The great hall at Nottingham castle was bustling with activity. Two farmers had brought a dispute to the sheriff over the ownership of a cow.

'I've owned the beast since she were a calf,' the first one stated.

'I bought her fair and square on market day,' countered the second.

'You stole her off my land!'

'You've been trying to get yer hands on 'er since two winters back!'

Jonas, the sheriff's newly appointed captain of the guard, motioned for the attendant soldiers to intervene and break up the building tension.

'Step back! There'll be no brawling here or you'll both lose a hand!' Jonas commanded. His men held the farmers in check with gusto.

'Oh, give me strength,' Robert de Rainault murmured from his position at the long table, at the end of the hall. 'Can this day get any worse?'

'I want what's mine!' the first farmer cried.

The sheriff raised a gloved hand as the second was about to respond. 'There'll be no shouting from either of you. You...' He pointed to the first farmer. 'You bred the animal?'

'Yes, my Lord Sheriff.'

'And you,' continued the sheriff, motioning to the second, 'you bought the animal?'

'That is correct, my Lord.'

'Both of you claim ownership. Neither of you will stand down. This leaves only one outcome.'

The farmers looked at their sheriff before glancing nervously at each other.

'Order your men back, Captain.' The sheriff stared at the two arguers. 'By the power vested in me by his Highness King John, I hereby decree that the cow is *mine*. Captain, bring it in for slaughter. We will feast on it tonight.'

The farmers were aghast, but the look the sheriff shot them made them back down almost immediately.

As they were being escorted out by Jonas and his men, the large hall door swung open and a figure stormed in.

In the smoky haze, de Rainault couldn't initially make out who it was: a man, certainly, from his stature. Tall, with blonde hair under a chainmail hood; wearing a black and grey tunic over which more chainmail hung. The tabard was ripped and stained with all manner of things.

As the man worked his way through the slowly dispersing throng, pushing his headgear back, de Rainault's mouth dropped open.

It couldn't be! Could it?

But it was.

The respective gaze of each was fixed upon the other. It was not a look of respect or admiration, or even of unspoken familiarity. It was a look of resignation, of frustrated acceptance.

The newcomer came to de Rainault's table and dropped a heavy bag of coins upon it.

The sheriff looked at the bag then back to the deliverer.

'Gisburne! As I live and breathe!'

CHAPTER 2

'And there I was hoping you'd expired in a field somewhere.'

'I take it you were not told of my return, Sheriff?' Gisburne spoke with a new boldness to his tone.

'Should I have been?' De Rainault stood as he called across the table to Jonas. 'Captain, it seems someone is standing in your place... or are *you* standing in *his*?'

'I informed your brother. I assumed he'd tell you.'

'Assumed, Gisburne?' De Rainault circled his erstwhile deputy. 'You are very sure of yourself. Has your time in Normandy given you the courage previously lacking?'

'I am not afraid of anything, my Lord.'

'Glad to hear it.' De Rainault clapped his hands once. It was enough to engage a servant, who scurried towards him. 'Wine. Let's *celebrate* this joyous return. And no, my beloved brother did not tell me of your return. Perhaps he didn't think it important.'

As Jonas reached the high table, he glared at Gisburne. 'Is Sir Guy staying long, my Lord? Shall I order the maids to prepare his chambers?'

'How about it, Gisburne? Is this a flying visit or are we to benefit from your gracious presence a little longer?'

Gisburne looked between de Rainault and Jonas. 'My legation in Normandy is now complete.'

The sheriff returned to his seat. Gisburne remained standing. The servant had returned with wine and goblets. 'And you want your old job back, is that it?'

'My Lord...' Jonas began.

'I have already filled the vacancy,' de Rainault smiled. 'The captain here is as equally adept as you were in fulfilling that capacity.'

'Surely my experience and longevity overrule any need for a replacement?' Gisburne motioned to the bag. 'A token of my loyalty.'

'Are you buying your way back in?'

'Not at all, my Lord. Consider it a gift.'

'That's most generous. Don't you agree, Captain?'

'Most generous,' Jonas murmured.

'Speak up!'

'Most generous, my Lord,' Jonas said loudly.

'I don't ever recall *you* bringing such gifts.' De Rainault was enjoying taunting Jonas while holding Gisburne at arm's length.

Leaning back in his chair, De Rainault sipped from his goblet of wine, letting the spices wash over his tongue as he considered the situation. He had always benefitted from Gisburne's brawn, blundering though it could be. Jonas, however, was stolid, regimented, and occasionally unable to act impulsively. He was young, still learning, still malleable, whereas Gisburne was seasoned; more now than ever. Perhaps it *would* be useful to have him back.

As he pondered, the sheriff noticed that Sir Guy remained perfectly still, as if waiting to pounce. Jonas however, seemed uncomfortable.

'Sit next to me, Gisburne. Drink with me.'

Gisburne breathed out and raised an eyebrow to Jonas, who had never been given the opportunity to sit at the sheriff's table.

Scowling, the captain moved back into the haze as the hall door opened once again.

'More surprises?' sighed de Rainault.

'Brother! I will have words with you.' The blur of purple cloth as Abbot Hugo stormed through the great hall abruptly stopped as he reached the table. 'Gisburne is...'

'Back, brother? Yes. I know.'

***

Sir Guy of Gisburne stared out across the fields and woodlands from his chambers high up in one of the towers of Nottingham castle, before turning to unpack his meagre belongings. Laying out his shaving knife, a leather strap to sharpen it with and a few trinkets sourced from some local markets, he considered the bitter sweetness of being back in the only place he'd ever truly called home.

It was calmer here than Normandy, where there was no respite from battle, where moments of solitude could never be found. He knew that the sheriff would not make his life easier but, by God, it was a damn sight more palatable than seeing death every day.

His heavy chainmail fell from his shoulders with a thud. As he stepped over it, an ochre glint amongst its links catching his eye. Kneeling, he pulled at a ragged piece of cloth, tugging as it caught on the mail, turning it over in his battle-sore hands as it came free. It was as wide as his palms and in its centre a large sun embroidered in gold. He smiled, nodding to himself as he tucked it out of sight between the blankets on his narrow cot.

Removing the rest of his garments, Guy moved to his chamber, and made ready to take to the bath the maidservants had prepared for him. He was about to lower himself into the steaming scented water when a rapping came at his door. Assuming it was the maids, he bade them enter.

'Sir Guy,' Jonas said as he crossed the threshold.

'Captain,' Gisburne replied, 'what do you want? Can't you see I'm bathing?'

Jonas looked over Gisburne's head, uncomfortable at having been sent on an errand boy's task. 'My Lord Sheriff demands your presence in his chambers.'

'Does he now?' Gisburne sat deeper into the water, enjoying the heat on his tired bones. 'Tell me, Captain. How did you get *my* position?'

'I...'

'Come on!'

Jonas frowned. This Sir Guy, this apparent oaf that the sheriff had complained about constantly in his absence, had so much bile for, sounded not unlike de Rainault himself. Perhaps that was why there was permanent animosity between them: the sheriff had moulded Gisburne into a version of himself.

'I was employed by the Abbot Hugo some time ago to entrap Robin Hood's men.'

'I take it you weren't successful.'

'About as successful as you ever were, Sir Guy.'

Gisburne looked Jonas directly in the eye. 'Do not attempt to cross me, Captain. I am back now and you will do as I say. Tell the sheriff I will be there as soon as I am done here.'

Jonas gritted his teeth, resenting having to acknowledge Gisburne's superiority. 'Right away, Sir Guy.'

'Oh, and Jonas...'

Jonas turned back into the room, his hand clutching the lip of the door. 'Yes, Sir Guy?'

'What happened to the sheriff's *other* Captain of the Guard? Flynn, wasn't it?'

'I believe he has been given duties elsewhere. Shall I inform him you wish to see him?'

'No, Jonas. That will be quite alright.'

With that, Jonas nodded curtly and went to deliver the reply to the sheriff.

***

'You took your time, you insolent wretch.' De Rainault scowled at Gisburne from where he lay on his luxurious bed, having his toenails cut by a manservant.

'I am sorry, my Lord.'

At the sheriff's table, by the open fireplace, Hugo sat eating some fresh fruit. Gisburne acknowledged the abbot as he asked the sheriff, 'What can I do for you?'

'Did you hear that, Hugo? He wants to know what *he* can do for *us*! It's as if we can't do without him. Ouch!' De Rainault kicked out at his servant. 'Do that again and I'll have your feet cut off.'

'Sounds like Normandy *has* given you a streak of a back bone, Guy,' scoffed the abbot.

'We have a plan to capture the outlaws,' said Robert de Rainault, keeping a close watch on the servant and his wandering clippers.

Another one? 'Shall I summon the men, my Lord Sheriff?'

'Not straight away. But they can certainly form some of your wedding party.'

'My...my *what*?' Gisburne stepped back, aghast.

'Don't look so terrified, Gisburne. Word has reached us that John Little plans to marry a wench from Wickham.'

'You, Gisburne,' cut in Hugo, 'are going to marry her instead.'

'But I don't *want* to get married, my Lords.'

'What's wrong with you, man?' asked Hugo. 'Of course you want to get married.'

'I *really* don't, my Lords.'

'Oh, for goodness sake!' Hugo raised his hands to heaven, 'Brother, you speak to him.'

'Hugo here,' the sheriff switched his full attention to Gisburne as the servant finished his task and left the room, 'has decided that you should go to Wickham, bring the woman Meg here, and marry her in the great hall.'

'To what end, my Lords? You have heard, I take it, of the planned interdict from Rome?'

'Of course we have!' Hugo snapped, 'That's why we must do this straight away. Before the Pope has his way and closes the churches. The marriage will be announced far and wide, as soon as possible. We'll also let it be known that the castle gates will be opened to all who wish to attend.'

The sheriff grunted, 'Hugo believes the people will want to celebrate your wonderful day with you. I can't imagine anything worse, myself.'

Gisburne nodded, beginning to understand what the de Rainault brothers had in mind. 'Robin Hood and his men will infiltrate the wedding and try to rescue the woman.'

'Good God, Robert, I do believe Gisburne has come back from Normandy with some common sense.'

The sheriff sat up, his expression eager at the thought of finally putting an end to Robin Hood's reign in Sherwood. 'The outlaws will be together and we can take them all at once. Your men will dress as guests and mingle with the masses so that the trap can be sprung.'

'I would suggest, my Lords, that we have some guards clearly visible as well. A total absence of guards would arouse suspicion.' Gisburne knew he had no choice but still couldn't help himself by finishing, 'I really do *not* want to get married, my Lords.'

De Rainault sneered as he got to his feet. 'You are getting married, Gisburne, or people will start to talk.'

'You know the outlaws will attempt to rescue her before you even get close to having to go through with the ceremony.' The abbot sounded less reassuring than Gisburne would have liked.

Suspecting the sheriff would insist on the service going to its conclusion, just to see the look on his face, Sir Guy ventured, 'Don't I at least get to consummate it?'

'For pity's sake,' said De Rainault, 'she's a serf! Anyway, you were dead against it a moment ago. It's just a charade. You'll be faking it.'

Hugo mumbled into his goblet of wine. 'Which is exactly what that wench would do if you got that far.'

CHAPTER 3

'Make sure you bring your shoes,' John said to Much as they unloaded a sack of grain from a cart in the centre of Wickham village.

'Why would I *not* bring my shoes?' Much was puzzled.

'It's tradition.'

'What is? Wearing shoes at a wedding?'

'No, not wearing them. To throw at the bridesmaids.'

'He's teasing you, Much,' laughed Marion as she sat outside Edward's home, weaving together a garland of flowers and herbs. 'It's traditional for the bride to throw shoes at her bridesmaids to see who will get married next. I don't know why they don't just throw flowers. That would be much gentler.'

'Oh,' responded Much, not quite seeing what the joke was. 'Where do you want this?'

Marion looked at the sack by Much's feet and the three others on the cart. 'They can go to Edward in the barn. I think one of them contains herbs for brewing. We'll need to get them started now if they're to be ready for the toasts by the time Meg has married her favourite outlaw.'

'Marion! Marion!' Meg's voice came from Edward's home, from where she was preparing to start married life.

'Coming Meg!' Marion called back. 'Can I leave you two to get this all sorted?'

'Of course,' said John.

As Marion moved away to see what Meg wanted, he leant towards Much conspiratorially. 'A warning, lad. This is what being married is like. Always being told what to do.'

'But you don't like being told what to do, so why are you getting married?'

'Perhaps I like being told what to do by Meg?' John smiled.

'Robin and Marion aren't married.' Much watched Marion head towards Edward's home. 'Does that mean Robin doesn't like her telling him what to do?'

'Maybe one day he will.'

'I don't think I'd like that, John, having to do what a girl says all the time.' But Much frowned then, as a thought crossed his mind. He shook it away but John caught his consternation.

'What's up?'

'It's…it's nothing.'

John put a wide hand on his friend's shoulder. 'It's *something*. What is it?'

Much looked up at John and leant against the cart. 'Just stupid thoughts.'

'Stupid thoughts aren't always as stupid as you think.'

Much sighed. 'I was thinking of Kate.'

'Kate of Papplewick?'

The young outlaw nodded. 'Yes.'

'She's not a stupid thought at all.'

What seemed like ages ago, and yet also felt like only yesterday to Much, he had spent a whole year getting to know Kate. She'd been a girl Robin had instructed him to meet with once a month, to swap any information about the sheriff or the local area that had reached her village, in return for money or food. He'd resented the task at first, having to travel, whatever the weather, to a specific meeting place very four weeks. It was only as the days turned into weeks, and the weeks into months that he'd realised they'd fallen in love.

'If she'd survived, you would have liked to have been told what to do by her, perhaps?' John, for all his gruffness and inelegance, could occasionally be very astute.

Much mumbled as he looked at his feet. 'I would have liked that very much.'

'Then you understand why I want Meg to tell *me* what to do, lad.' He handed Much his quarterstaff and hauled the three sacks at once onto his back. 'Come on, let's get these indoors. I think it's going to rain.'

***

Meg was sitting on a stool staring at her hands when Marion came through the door.

'Why are you sitting in here on your own?'

'Oh, Marion…' Meg, her hair in disarray and her elfin face puckered, burst into tears.

Marion rushed to her side. 'Whatever's the matter?'

Meg tried to answer, but no words would form through her sobs, she was acting as if her very existence was about to be extinguished.

No matter how much Marion soothed her, telling Meg everything would be fine and that John was a good man who would do everything he could to keep her safe and happy, her friend was inconsolable. Meg simply blinked up at Marion through puffy eyes, crying until there were no tears left and her exhausted sobs finally lapsed into the silence of sleep.

It was late in the afternoon when Meg awoke. Marion had stayed by her side, finishing the garlands, preparing Meg's clothing and stirring a small pot of mead over the fire.

'Marion…'

'Hello, Meg. How are you feeling?'

'I'm sorry.'

'Don't be. There's no need. Everyone feels like that sometimes. Marriage is a big step.'

'Did…did *you*?'

Marion rested the ladle in the pot of mead. Being married came with the danger of one day becoming a widow, which was exactly what Marion was. She'd come to terms with it, found herself loved by another and so the memory of being the wife to Robin of Loxley, while still lingering, was not as painful as it used to be.

'In a way, yes,' Marion confirmed. 'I was nervous. We both were. But we loved each other very much. He was devoted to me and I him.'

'And you were always together.'

'Yes,' Marion smiled. 'For as long as we were meant to be.'

Meg sat up, tucking her knees under her chin. Marion gave her a small tankard filled with the mead. Meg sipped at it and placed it on the stool. 'But you were *together*.'

'We were husband and wife. Of course we were.'

'What was it like when he… you know…'

'Died?' Marion whispered and she swallowed back an internal sigh. 'My whole world collapsed. He was everything to me. Everything we stood for, the life we had given ourselves and all we did for the oppressed, the poor. Suddenly it was all for nothing, or so I thought. But his legacy lives on. I moved on. I understood that nothing was ever forgotten. And here we are – still in Sherwood, still fighting for what he believed in. And now I'm loved by Robert…by *Robin*.'

'But John won't stop being in Sherwood. And I won't live in Sherwood neither.'

'John is...'

'An outlaw? Yes. Like Robin. Like you. But I'm not.' Meg stared at the ash in the fire. 'He'll go out every day. He'll be with you all. And I'll be sitting at home wondering if he'll come back alive.'

Marion placed a hand on Meg's knee and shuffled up next to her. 'You've known John for a long time. He's always come back to you.'

'But when we're married it will be different.'

'Have you told him how you feel?'

'Yes. We had words about it some time back.'

'And what did he say?'

'That I shouldn't worry, that there's nothing to fear when he's around.'

'There you go then.'

'But what happens when he's *not* around? Whether it be for a day, a night, or forever more? I dream of us having land in Wickham, settling down properly, mebbe having littluns.'

Marion sighed, 'Well, we can't do this forever, running around Sherwood saving everyone. So perhaps in time, John's calling will change. He'll know when the time is right and then you'll have him by your side always. Anyway...' Marion stood, stretching her back, '...time's getting on. Tomorrow you'll be a married woman! Let's see what that fiancé of yours is up to.'

Marion opened the door and peered outside. There was no one around.

It wasn't dark and the rain that had threatened earlier hadn't come, yet something told her she should be on her guard.

Meg sensed her concern and came up to her, peering around her shoulder. 'Where is everybody?'

'That's what I'd like to know,' Marion breathed.

'John!' Meg suddenly called out. 'Joh—'

Marion clamped a hand over Meg's mouth. 'Quiet!' she hissed between her teeth, dragging her friend back within and closing the door.

'But John will know what's wrong,' Meg said, pushing Marion away. 'He'll be here in a while.'

'Shhh.... no one's around. John's not... around.'

Meg realised what Marion meant, why she had tailed off in her reply.

There's nothing to fear when he's around

'Marion of Leaford!' The shout echoed across the deserted village.

Marion raised her hand to keep Meg quiet. She leant an ear to the door to see if she could recognise the voice. She could hear the shuffled of feet as the voice came again.

'We know you're here. Come out or Wickham will suffer!'

That sounds like Gisburne! But he's in Normandy. Isn't he?

Marion dared take a peek through a crack in the door. She could see right across Wickham to the line of trees that led into the forest on the other side.

In the very centre of the village, with Edward on his knees, a sword to his throat, Sir Guy of Gisburne stood, his unmistakeable blonde hair atop a scowling face.

Marion turned back to Meg. 'You stay here. It's me they're after.'

Meg went to object but Marion shook her head. Grabbing her long bow and quiver on the way out, an arrow was already nocked by the time she exited Edwards' home.

The moment Marion appeared, from out of every house, stepped Gisburne's men; all fully armed and each with a villager captive.

Marion swung her arrow around in defiance, even though she knew she couldn't save a single hostage alone.

Where the hell are John and Much?

'It is remiss of your wolfshead friends to leave you solely in charge of Wickham's safety.' Gisburne taunted.

John and Much must be hiding somewhere if Gisburne thinks I'm alone.

'What makes you say that?' Marion responded. 'We're all around you. You just can't see us.'

'A bold statement,' Gisburne said. 'But Edward here swore on his son's life that you were alone in there. No other outlaws. Isn't that right?'

'Yes… yes,' said Edward, wincing as Gisburne increased the pressure at his throat.

From behind Gisburne stepped Jonas, with Matthew, Edward's son, bound and gagged like an animal.

'Don't hurt my boy…' Edward wheezed.

Marion looked at Matthew then Edward, considering for a moment whether to lower her weapon. If she shot Jonas, Matthew would be able to flee, even if Edward couldn't escape. 'What do you want with me?'

'Lower your weapon Lady Wolfshead, and I will tell you,' called Gisburne.

Behind Gisburne, beyond Jonas, Marion suddenly spotted a comforting sight. Much and John were hiding behind the line of trees that formed the boundary between Sherwood and Wickham.

Hope stirring in her, Marion called back. 'If you and your men lower your weapons too, then I'll come quietly.'

CHAPTER 4

Jonas turned to Gisburne, nervous sweat trickling down his neck. 'It's a trick, my Lord.'

'Of course it's a trick,' Gisburne replied. 'The others with be here somewhere, in hiding.'

'Do we lower our weapons?'

'No.' Gisburne pulled at Edward, so he was stood directly before him. 'She won't try to kill any of us. She won't run the risk of us not slitting the villager's throats.'

'Then let's just slit their throats and be done with it.' Jonas shrugged.

Gisburne shook his head. 'Our orders are to bring the woman in, not slaughter a village. The sheriff can have that blood on his hands if he so wishes. I'm not having it on mine. As soon as we hurt these people the outlaws will come screaming out of the forest.'

'But, my Lord,' Jonas said, 'there are more of us than them. They'll be no match for us.'

Gisburne shot Jonas a look that told him to quieten down. He turned back to Marion, detecting a slight tremble in her grip. Was she alone after all? Was that why she seemed nervous?

***

Marion's arms were beginning to shake. She had to maintain the pretence that she was the only outlaw in Wickham. Taking a deep breath, she closed her eyes for a split second to calm her mind, re-focus on holding the bow and nocked arrow as confidently as she could.

Without making it obvious she was doing so, she watched as John and

Much split up and creep to either side of the village entrance, silently taking down a handful of Gisburne's men in the process. She needed to hold Gisburne's attention for just a little longer…

'Are we going to stand here all evening, Sir Guy?' she taunted. 'I have better things to do.'

Two more men down.

'We can stay here as long as is needed before you see sense and surrender.'

'I said already that I would come quietly. But you haven't yet lowered your weapons or let the villagers go.'

'Do you think me stupid?'

'I think you're afraid of a solitary woman, severely outnumbered by you, standing before you with a long-bow.'

Three more men.

'Why are you here alone?'

Before she could answer, John and Much rushed forward on silent feet, until they were behind Jonas and Gisburne.

'Surprise…' John whispered in Gisburne's ear.

In shock, Gisburne whirled around, releasing his hold on Edward just as Jonas did dropped Matthew. Each man raised their swords to parry John's quarterstaff and Much's dagger.

'Run, boy!' shouted Edward to his son, unsheathing a hidden knife from his belt. He lunged for Jonas, slashing the captain of the guard across his thigh.

Jonas cried out and stumbled, as Matthew, stumbling within the restrictions of his bindings, headed for Marion.

Much dashed towards a couple of the soldiers holding two villagers hostage. Screaming a banshee cry of rage as he ran, Much lunged at the guards as they drew their weapons.

As the other soldiers realised what was happening, they joined in the fight, leaving the villagers free to huddle together for safety with Matthew and Edward.

Marion held her ground, releasing arrow after arrow. She'd already felled four of Gisburne's men, giving some space for Much and John to fend off Jonas' and Gisburne's attacks, when a new sense that something wasn't right trickled down her spine.

Gisburne, Jonas and the soldiers, while readily engaging in combat with John and Much, seemed lacklustre in their efforts, half-hearted in attacking and unconcerned that the villagers were free. Nevertheless, the outlaws kept up the fight, determined that Sir Guy wouldn't not take Marion.

A sudden scream stopped John in his tracks; the sound draining the colour from his face.

He spun around, and to his horror saw some soldiers carrying a struggling, kicking and spitting Meg, throwing her into a waiting caged wagon. They must have snuck around to the rear of Edward's house, knowing the outlaws were focused on Gisburne and Jonas.

'Meg!' he roared.

Marion spun around to give chase, but another soldier sprinted across the clearing, striking her hard on the side of the head, leaving Marion unconscious and sprawled in the dirt.

By the time John had realised what was happening, the wagon, the remaining soldiers and Jonas and Gisburne had all departed, leaving John and Much in the centre of Wickham, stunned, tired and furious.

***

There was an anger in John that Robin hadn't witnessed before, and he had killed by the man's side.

It was late afternoon by the time they'd returned to Sherwood. Lifting an unconscious Marion from the horse he'd shared with her, John gently lowered her to the ground and Much hurried to find Tuck.

'What happened, John?' Robin stoked Marion's face as he looked up at his friend.

'Gisburne…' John growled, spittle flecking his beard.

'Gisburne?' Robin groaned. 'He is back, then. I'd heard rumours he'd been seen around Nottingham.'

'Aye, he's back. He tricked us.' John glared at Robin. 'They took Meg.'

'Meg? But it was Marion they were after.'

'Aye, that's what Herne told you, was it? Well he was wrong.'

'Herne isn't ever…' Robin didn't have the chance to finish his sentence. John had already stomped off into the gloom, striking trees and the undergrowth with his quarterstaff as he went.

Tuck bustled over to Marion, wiping her brow as Robin asked, 'Will she be alright?'

Tuck felt Marion's scalp through her thick hair and checked her neck for any swelling. 'She'll have a bit of a sore head for a day or so, but she'll be alright.'

'Should we sit her up?'

'No, let her rest where she is. Much…some furs, please.'

Robin was thoughtful as Much helped Tuck make Marion comfortable.

'How could I have got that wrong, Tuck? I was convinced it was Marion Herne was talking about.'

'Herne only interprets what he foresees. Can any of us truly and clearly tell the future? Even him?'

'He's rarely wrong!'

'That's not what I meant, Robin.' Tuck kept his eyes on his patient. 'He told you a maiden would need us to rescue them, and that we would all be there to be captured. You assumed it was Marion.'

Robin nodded, hating how much trouble his incorrect assumption had caused. 'Poor John.'

'Aye. He's a big lump of a man but he has a heart.'

Robin placed a hand on Marion's side. 'Marion could have taken care of herself, but Meg…she must be terrified. We need to rescue her.'

Will and Nasir came into their camp.

'John ain't listenin' to me,' Will was agitated. 'Says he's going to go get Meg back himself. Won't let me go instead.'

'John is upset, Will. He'll come around soon,' said Robin.

'Yeah, but what if he goes off? He ain't thinking straight. He'll get himself killed.'

'You act with your heart, also,' Nasir observed.

'Yeah, I'm used to it though. Keeps me goin'. John's no. He might do somethin' stupid.'

'Which direction did he go in?' asked Robin.

'Darkmere,' replied Nasir.

'That's not the way to Nottingham,' pointed out Will.

'No.' Robin looked concerned. 'He's heading for Herne.'

***

Years of moving through Sherwood as if he were a ghost, using his knowledge of the trees as hiding place or shelter… all that knowledge deserted John as he crashed through the night.

John had never loved anyone but Meg. He'd never met anyone else like her. He could hear his blood rushing through his ears, her panicked scream echoing in the background. The tightness in his chest was almost suffocating as his mind focused on just one thing.

Herne and Robin had been wrong.

While they were distracted, Gisburne's men had taken Meg from under their very noses. He was going to confront Herne and ask him what he was going to do about it.

His quarterstaff clearing his path, John ignored the chill around his shoulders. He knew Sherwood intimately; he'd been this way untold times, but suddenly he stopped, realising he needed to check his surroundings.

It was left… no, right… no, straight on. Or should he go back the way he'd come?

John growled to himself and tried to think.

Meg. It's because I can't stop thinking about Meg. Concentrate!

He remained still and thought hard, but the trees all looked the same. He was lost.

No. I'm not lost.

Determined to get back on the right path, he closed his eyes and breathed deeply. He *knew* Sherwood. It was impossible that he could have strayed off his path.

As he opened his eyes to continue his journey, a thick mist that hadn't been there a moment ago, collected around his ankles, obscuring the ferns and bracken across the forest's floor.

John lifted his quarterstaff. 'Who's there?'

There was no one in sight, but John was convinced someone was there. He spun around. He was alone in the darkness but there was a voice in his head. A voice than imprinted itself over his own thoughts.

Wolfshead… outlaw…

Do you fear me, John Little of Hathersage?

A crack of lightening made John duck instinctively. As he pulled himself back up to his full height, there, a few yards away from him, haloed by light and mist, was Herne the Hunter.

'Do not approach me in anger, John Little,' the vision boomed, antlers swinging towards him.

'I… I want to know why Meg has been taken,' John said.

'The Hooded Man knows of what you speak.'

'He told us that *you* told him we'd all be captured. He didn't say why Meg is involved. She's not an outlaw. She should still be in Wickham. She should be safe!'

'Take heed, John Little. Where there is safety is also danger. By coming here you have weakened the resolve.'

'I'm not weak!' shouted John.

'Captured all or captured none. So must it be.'

A brilliant flash of light in the darkness and John fell backwards, the cushion of the forest floor holding him close as the mist cleared and the moon broke through the trees.

He was alone once more.

CHAPTER 5

It was a chilly dark morning as the small phalanx of soldiers, protecting a team of huntsmen, moved out of Nottingham castle and north towards Calvretone. Mounted at its head were Jonas and Flynn.

'Capture all of them, or capture none of them,' Jonas was saying. 'Why can't we just pick them off one by one instead? That would break their ranks, make them weaker.'

His mutterings caused murmured ripples through the marching soldiers behind them.

'That's not the way the sheriff wants it,' replied Flynn. 'You've been with us long enough already to know that.'

'But it doesn't make any sense.'

'Now that Sir Guy is back, you don't have to worry anymore. Let them upstairs do the worrying about the outlaws,' Flynn said, motioning with a nod of his head back in the general direction of the castle.

That was something else that was bothering Jonas. Why *had* Gisburne returned?

Earlier, keen to find out the answer to that question, he'd waited until Flynn and his men had gone to prepare the horses before going to hunt wild boar for the wedding feast, before heading towards Gisburne's chambers.

With the woman from Wickham safely locked away in her own room and the sheriff, Gisburne and the abbot busy elsewhere, Jonas had moved through the castle easily enough. No one had questioned him or stopped him on his journey to Gisburne's chamber door.

He knocked with determination.

Had Gisburne answered, Jonas would have simply asked if he was attending the boar hunt. As it was, no response came from within so Jonas tried the latch. It was unlocked and the chambers opened up before him.

It hadn't taken long for Jonas to search the place in his quest to find anything that might indicate why Sir Guy had returned. The chambers were meagre and sparse and it seemed, even for his knighthood, Gisburne owned very little. Perhaps that was why he'd returned? Gisburne knew he would have employment, a roof over his head, a—

Something then caught Jonas' eye, something half-concealed under the blankets that made up Gisburne's bed and Jonas tugged at it. It was a piece of cloth, no bigger than a hand, with a gold sun emblazoned across one side. It obviously meant something to Sir Guy for it to have been hidden in his private room, albeit not very well. Possibly a memento from his time in Normandy. Or a keepsake of a fallen enemy, perhaps?

Jonas heard the clatter of booted feet going past the door so stuffed the material under his own tunic.

It was still with him now as the hunting procession joined the Ollerton road.

Rumour had it that there were any number of boars to be had in Calvretone and the sheriff's table would be well stocked with succulent roasted park. He hoped the kitchens had mastered the art of crackling; the last cook seemed to have little or no understanding of how to do it properly.

The men had been eager to attend the hunt. It made a pleasant change to be out of the sheriff's line of fire, and Jonas was determined to make sure the day would be enjoyable for them. Tomorrow would be a different story. He knew from the accounts given to him by Flynn, and his own experience, that coming up against Robin Hood and his men was not something to be approached lightly.

As the Ollerton road continued northwards, Jonas and Flynn guided their men east at Woodthorpe, past the site of an old Viking settlement and on to the woodland that touched Calvretone itself.

Setting up a temporary base, the four professional hunters that accompanied the soldiers, made themselves comfortable as they prepared for a morning of hunting. Jonas and Flynn joined them, removing the burden of their chainmail behind as they left their horses resting at the camp.

Swords striking shields, the soldiers, stretched along a line, moved with deliberate slowness through the trees, aiming to scare the boar into the open. Soon they could hear the undergrowth rustle as not just wild pigs scattered out of the way. Weasels, rabbits and even the occasional pheasant fled from the noise.

Seeing some boar a few yards away, two huntsmen broke off, silencing the soldiers. Jonas crouched low, pulling Flynn down with him.

'This reminds me of when I was a boy. My uncle used to take me with him to catch our supper,' he whispered. A huntsman glared at him, as Jonas' voice sent a boar scampering in the opposite direction.

'If we go back to Nottingham without the sheriff's wedding supper, it'll be us on the spit,' responded Flynn, his voice quieter still.

Suddenly a boar came darting towards them, catching Flynn off guard. He was surprised at how fast they were. Their tusks, as they flashed by, seemed terrifyingly sharp. Flynn stumbled into Jonas who laughed.

The huntsmen gave chase, arrows whistling through the air as the boars squealed in panic. Jonas hauled Flynn up and they followed, but they didn't see the second beast hurtle up behind them. Flynn was knocked off his feet once more and crashed into Jonas, who spun around just as the boar twisted itself back and charged towards to teetering captain.

The tusks had embedded themselves in Jonas' thigh before anyone realised what was happening. The captain cried out, falling backwards, as the boar charged for a third time, gouging into Jonas' abdomen before a huntsman could bring the creature to its knees.

Jonas gasped in agony as Flynn rushed to support his head. Just as he stared down in horror at his comrade's mangled stomach, a great cry echoed through the trees.

'What the...' began Flynn.

One of the huntsmen came to a halt. 'A man... He's running through the woods.'

'A poacher?'

'No. He's not got a long-bow.'

'My Lords!' called a soldier, trotting towards them, his stomach churning as he saw Jonas. 'An... an outlaw!'

'Outlaw?' This was a fine time to stumble across a wolfshead, Flynn cursed, looking back at Jonas' wounds. The captain was gasping for air between bouts of pain. The boar had all but disembowelled him.

'He has a quarterstaff.'

Jonas grimaced and grabbed Flynn's arm. 'The one they call Little John...'

'Ease yourself, Jonas.'

'Leave me. Get the outlaw.'

'You must rest. Your wounds...'

'They...they...' Jonas sagged back. 'A feast *and* an outlaw... You will be in good favour with the... the sheri...'

Whether he had fallen unconscious or worse, Flynn didn't know but the outlaw had roared again, and Flynn told the huntsman to stay with Jonas.

Flynn unsheathed his sword and followed the soldier. In a small clearing, his men had Little John surrounded. The outlaw seemed to be in pain and Flynn saw a trickle of blood at the man's left wrist.

'Give it up, wolfshead!' Flynn called out but John swung out with his staff.

A soldier lunged at John from behind, knocking him to the ground. Flynn motioned for the other men to dive in and before long John was smothered in a gamut of arms, legs, swords and shields.

'Get off me! Get off me!' John roared but his injured wrist, a lucky strike from one of the soldier's swords, didn't allow him the purchase he needed and found he couldn't throw the soldiers off.

Flynn was relieved. As far as he could see from an initial glance, none of the soldiers or the huntsmen had been injured in the fight, save for a few bruises. Jonas, on the other hand, was in a bad way. If he survived the journey back to Nottingham, there was a good chance he wouldn't see the next sunrise.

***

John breathed heavily as his hands and arms were tied behind his back. He'd been bound for Nottingham, determined to rescue Meg alone. He knew now how stupid that idea had been, and he had no way of getting a message to Robin and the others. He just hoped that they would work out where he'd been heading.

Remaining silent as he was hauled to his feet and attached to one of two horses and told to wait, John's thoughts of successfully rescuing Meg crumbled to dust.

CHAPTER 6

In Nottingham castle's great hall, the sheriff's legs were beginning to ache. He'd been standing for what seemed like hours, rooted to one spot, while the artist sketched his portrait.

'You haven't even got your paints out yet, you hedge-born mandrake mymmerkin,' scowled the sheriff. 'How long it this going to go on for? And Gisburne...'

'Yes, my Lord?'

'Stop prowling.'

'I still don't like this plan of yours,' Gisburne replied.

'Don't you?' The sheriff shrugged. 'That's not really my concern.'

'Would you mind keeping still, my Lord Sheriff?' asked the painter gingerly.

'What?' De Rainault glared at the artist, a mousey-looking individual called Piers with permanently stained fingers and a nervous tic in one eye.

'You need to keep still,' Piers repeated timidly, 'so I can paint you accurately.'

'*You* need to hurry up!' spat de Rainault as he twisted back towards Gisburne. 'I've sent messengers out already inviting everyone to the nuptials, Gisburne. This *will* happen the day after tomorrow. Your blushing bride is already safely ensconced in her chambers and your men should be back with the wedding supper soon.'

'My Lord...p-please...' The artist stammered, his plea breaking off as the sheriff glared at him, before purposely reaching out for his goblet of wine, going to great lengths to take his time in drinking it.

Gisburne moved forward to grab a leg of lamb from the table and getting in Piers' way.

'My *Lords*...'

'Ha! Your turn now for the wrath of our little friend, here,' de Rainault said, throwing the goblet across the hall. 'Whose idea was this painting anyway?'

'Your brother's, my Lord Sheriff,' Gisburne replied. 'Although, I'd have thought it would make more sense to have the groom's portrait painted rather than the...the...'

'Go on, say it! The best man!' De Rainault snorted at the notion. 'I believe the best man's duty is to seek out and capture a bride from a neighbouring community. I think I performed that function successfully.'

'It was Abbot Hugo's plan,' Sir Guy reminded him. 'And I had to fetch her myself!'

'Well, there you go. It was my duty then to make sure you knew what you were getting. And I will gladly ask Piers here to paint your likeness. Then you can remember your wedding day for the rest of your miserable life.'

Gisburne thought about that for a moment and shook his head.

'I didn't think so,' sneered the sheriff.

Piers sighed as de Rainault switched his weight from one leg to the other. 'I fear I may have to start again, my Lord.'

'I fear you may be thrown off the battlements! Just get this thing done!'

'I ask you, my Lord, if you would be so kind as to sit still. It is difficult to paint when you do not hold a pose.'

'Ah!' called de Rainault as Hugo entered, the great wooden candelabra high above them swinging in the sudden breeze.

Piers shook his head in despair as the sheriff moved to greet his brother and knocked the canvas over.

'Going well, I see?' Hugo said. 'I thought you would have finished by now.'

'This imbecile you sent me can't paint an apple let alone a person.'

'I was informed he has flair.'

'He has about as much flair as an illiterate ploughman!' retorted the sheriff. 'Look at his hands! They could shovel dung easier rather than hold a brush!'

Piers fumbled for the canvas, dropping his brushes, knocking over his palette. The more the de Rainault brothers mocked him, the clumsier he became. Electing to adjust the position of the picture rather than ask its subject to move again, Piers swung the canvas around. But just as he moved, the sheriff walked forward, and Piers struck him straight in the middle of back. De Rainault sprawled to the stone floor, filthy hay and mud in his face.

Spluttering, indignant, raging, he clambered to his feet. 'Get out! Get out! Go paint yourself, you repetitive cretin!' The sheriff kicked Pier's as he scrambled to collect up his brushes in his haste to leave.

De Rainault glared at the spilt oils on the floor. 'And get this mess cleaned up! Gisburne!'

'Yes, my Lord?'

'You had better be sure your men can bring back enough boar from the hunt, or it will be your funeral, not your wedding!'

'They can always serve soup, my Lord,' Gisburne responded dryly.

'Are you trying to be funny?'

Gisburne raised an eyebrow, 'Not at all, my Lord. I just want it to be over and done with as quickly as possible. Soup is easy. Barely an inconvenience.'

The abbot threw Gisburne a look of derision. 'What will be an inconvenience is if you don't play along! This is an opportunity to dispose of those wolfsheads once and for all.'

'Hugo is right, Gisburne. If you don't like it then you shouldn't have slunk back from Normandy.' The sheriff demanded a nearby servant pour him some more wine. 'Guards, bring the Wickham wench here. Let's see if we can get St Dwynwen herself to somehow get some love blooming. Although we might need an exorcism looking at the expression on Gisburne's face.'

***

Only a few minutes later, Meg was brought into the hall. On seeing the sheriff, abbot and Gisburne, she spat at their feet.

'Charming,' said Gisburne. 'And you expect me to marry *that*?'

'Eh?' Meg looked between them. 'Oh…no, no, *no*.'

'Look at her, Gisburne! Your new bride! Is she not pretty? Is she not shapely? Is she not feisty?'

'I'll show you feisty, you weasel!' said Meg, kicking out towards the sheriff, causing the guards to hold her arms more firmly.

Robert de Rainault walked up to her, waited until she had stopped struggling, and then knocked her feet out from under her. She dropped to the floor like a puppet freed of its strings as the guards let go.

'She will not play her part,' Gisburne said. 'She will not go through with.'

'She doesn't have to. Only one of you does.'

'I ain't betrothed to this foppish fool!' Meg said from her position on the floor. Then she stood, fists clenched and looking as if she were about to punch them all.

'A wife with a mind of her own? Well, well, Gisburne,' the sheriff crowed, '…at least you'll be able to share hers rather than trying to find one for yourself!'

Gisburne glared at his superior. 'This plan is suicidal.'

'If you're saying that the plan to marry me is suicidal, then you're right!'

exclaimed Meg. 'You'll regret it when my John gets a-hold of you!'

Grabbing a chunk of bread from the table, de Rainault tore at it with his teeth, circling Meg as he chewed, taking in her wild hair and even wilder expression. 'Is that any way to talk to your fiancé's best man? I don't think so. What do you think, Gisburne? You should control your woman.'

'M-*my* woman...? I-I... don't...'

'Breathe, Gisburne!' The sheriff puffed out in despair. 'Don't worry, Meg. We'll get that stammer sorted before the big day, even if I have to use hot irons on his tongue.' He went back and sat in his ornate raised chair, his own personal throne from where he could look down at his subjects; at the serfs and peasants that made the place look unsightly. He couldn't abide any of them and the thought that the place would be jammed to the rafters with the scum on Gisburne's wedding day made him shudder.

'I'll not marry him!' Meg shouted. 'I'd rather...'

'Rather what, you wretched *puterelle*?' demanded de Rainault.

'I am not!' Meg responded. 'How dare you imply that I'm a—'

'You'll hang, woman, if you don't go through with this!'

'You brought me here and I haven't committed a crime. You've no right!'

'Rights? Shall I tell you about rights?'

Meg didn't break the sheriff's glare. 'I think you're about to.'

'There are no rights for people like you!'

'People like me?' Meg knew they needed her for some reason, specifically her, so found bravery in that fact. She wouldn't be harmed. At least not yet.

'Saxons...Pagans...the uncivilised. You forget who your masters are. If we hadn't rescued you all from yourselves, you'd still be living in caves!'

'Then why would people like *you* want to marry into people like us? I haven't got anything to offer you.'

'On the contrary, you have lots to offer us.'

'Like what? I've no chattels, no money. Nothing.'

'I would like to say what you have is priceless,' smiled the sheriff, 'but how much *is* a band of cut-throat wolfsheads worth these days?'

'Wolfsheads? You mean John and... and the others...' Meg looked down at her bare feet. She was a lure. Marrying Gisburne... it was a trap. 'They won't fall for it.'

'That's what I—'

'Enough, Gisburne!' said the sheriff.

'Your outlaw friends,' Hugo began, 'won't be able to stop themselves. They see Wickham's villagers as their own precious pets to fawn over, so to have one of them here, marrying into a knighthood, even if it *is* Gisburne... well, we expect them to be knocking at the castle gates at first light on your big day eager to rescue you.'

'You'll either marry Gisburne or you'll hang,' summarised the sheriff.

'Then, I'll...' Meg stood straight. She would remain defiant even to the last. She knew John would find a way to rescue her. All she had to do was bide her time. And to do that, she'd need to agree to this ridiculous marriage.

'I'll marry him.'

Gisburne's mouth dropped open in surprise as the doors to the great hall suddenly flew open and Flynn strode in, his gait strong and self-assured.

Behind him, with a chain at his throat, his wrists and ankles manacled like he was some sort of wild beast, was Little John.

He was bruised and battered and uncharacteristically subdued. A broken man, he looked Meg, his apology at being captured silent but obvious.

Meg knew then that all was lost.

CHAPTER 7

'Herne couldn't tell me where John has gone,' Robin stood with his friends in Wickham's main barn.

'Why not?' asked Will.

'He said that John's mind is clouded.'

'I'll tell you where he's gone. To get Meg! You don't need Herne to work that out!' Will oozed frustration. He was standing away from the group, leaning against a pillar, his arms folded over his chest. 'We should go to Nottingham now and get them both back.'

'No, Scarlet,' Robin said sternly.

'No?' Will thumped the pillar. 'You don't do nothin'. You sit and you talk.'

'Robin's right,' Marion nodded. 'If we all head there now, will be walking into an ambush.'

'Herne said we will all be captured if we go.' Robin turned to Nasir, who sat quietly on a pile of hay. 'What do you think, Nasir?'

The Saracen played a knife in his fingers as he spoke. 'The sheriff will expect us. We do not rescue them. That is *not* expected.'

'So we don't *all* go!' suggested Will. 'I'll go alone!'

'What do you think?' Robin asked the group.

Nasir's eyes narrowed, unconvinced.

'We can't expect you to break into Nottingham castle and rescue both John and Meg alone on your own,' Tuck wiped his brow as a ray of summer sunshine found its way through the barn's wooden slats.

'We can't expect any of us to do this alone.' Marion looked at Robin. 'But if Herne said we'd all be captured...'

'You're implying we should change his prophecy?' Robin was uncomfortable with what she was suggesting.

'Why not? It's happened before, hasn't it?'

'Has it?' Robin looked at Marion and his men. He sat back down on the hay. 'If it was one of us imprisoned in Nottingham...'

'It *is* one of us! John isn't thinking straight. I'm sure he's gone and got himself caught,' said Will.

'And we saw Gisburne take Meg!' added Much.

'So we do it in stages,' Will said. 'If they're expecting us all, then we will all go – just not at the same time!'

'Better idea.' Nasir nodded. 'We infiltrate.'

'If you're worried about going against Herne's vision, remember you said it was me that you all were to rescue.' Marion added, 'But it's not. It's Meg.'

'You're right, Little Flower.'

'I never said it was you, Marion,' Robin corrected her.

'You did, Robin,' Much muttered, not comfortable with contradicting his leader.

'I said it was a *maiden*, not Marion. I just *concluded* it was Marion.' Robin looked at the ground.

'You let Meg get caught!' chided Will.

'No, Will. I did not. How was I to know it was Meg that Herne was talking of? It just made sense that it would have been Marion. I wish I hadn't been wrong, but I was!'

'And we can't exactly protect all the other maidens we might know in case they get taken,' said Tuck. 'That would be impossible.'

Will growled under his breath, knowing Robin was right to have reached the conclusion he did and that Tuck spoke sense.

Edward entered the barn then, looking flustered. 'Robin, Marion, all of you... Soldiers, coming to the village.'

'What do they want now?' hissed Will, unsheathing his broadsword. He peered out through the partly open barn door and saw two armed soldiers from the castle emerging from the trees. They were flanking a younger man who seemed to be holding some form of instrument and a scroll.

'It's a trumpet,' Tuck said, looking around Will's shoulder.

'He's a messenger,' said Robin. 'Edward, you'd better go. We should stay here. If word gets back to the sheriff that you've been in our company again, that will cause you even more trouble.'

As Edward went out to see what the messenger had to say, Robin whispered to the others, 'I have a feeling we are meant to hear this.' With Albion at his hip, Robin pushed the door open a fraction, hoping they'd be able to make out what was said.

The messenger raised his trumpet to his lips and blew four simple notes, before he launched into his proclamation.

'Now hear this! Now hear this! It is decreed by the Lord High Sheriff of Nottingham, Robert de Rainault, appointed by His Royal Majesty King John, that all are welcome to join the sheriff and his household in Nottingham castle to celebrate the marriage of Sir Guy of Gisburne...'

'Who would be willing to marry him? I pity the poor wench who agreed to that!' Will called out, causing the messenger to glare across the village square towards the barn and the two soldiers to tighten their grip on the swords.

'Quiet, Will!' admonished Robin.

'...to celebrate,' the messenger continued, 'the marriage of Sir Guy of Gisburne...'

'Get on with it!'

'Will!' Marion kicked Scarlet's ankles.

'...to Meg of Wickham.'

Robin and his companions gasped as one.

'Oh, the poor child,' Tuck wheezed, marking the sign of the cross on himself.

'What did he say?' Will said, teeth gritted. 'What. Did. He. *Say*?'

'We all heard it, Will,' Robin responded quietly, laying a hand on his friend's arm, preventing him from charging out of the barn and attacking the messenger.

'The union will be as the cock crows in two mornings' time,' finished the messenger, before turning on the soles of his boots and leaving the village at speed.

Scarlet growled after him, 'I'll wring the cock's bloody neck!'

Robin kept a firm hold of Will's arm. 'John acted hastily and look what happened. We need to plan this properly.'

'We ain't got time! You heard 'im! Two days! Meg will be married to that snake in two days!'

Edward led them back into the barn. 'What can I do to help, Robin?'

The Hooded Man smiled and placed a hand on Edward's shoulder. 'Thank you. But I can't risk your life.'

'Meg is as much a daughter to me as she is a member of our village.'

'Aye, that's true, Robin' agreed Tuck. 'Edward raised her when her own mother died.'

'That I did, Robin,' said Edward, 'Meg's father, Durward, was killed when Loxley village was burnt. He had helped Ailric get everyone to safety before the sheriff cut him down.'

That second name was unfamiliar to Robin but it meant everything to Marion and the rest of the band. Edward nodded at her as she gave a sorrowful smile.

'I owe it to Durward. He was head of Wickham afore me, and he put his life before others to save them.'

'Then we'd be honoured if you would join us,' said Robin. 'Now, here's what we're going to do...'

***

The dungeon deep in the bowels of Nottingham castle was one of the worst places Little John had ever been in. He'd been imprisoned in it more than once already in his life and he always knew that there was the chance he would find himself back here. It hadn't been a shock to him when he was flung down the hole; the iron grate slammed and locked shut even before he'd had the chance to raise his head from the foul-smelling ground he'd landed on.

He'd been marched at speed from Calvretone, quipping to Flynn that it had been lucky they'd been headed in the same direction. The injured officer on the cart (John hadn't seen who it was) seemed to have been in bad shape and was quickly taken away into another part of the castle when they'd arrived.

Then he'd been dragged before the sheriff and his cronies like the common criminal they accused him of being. He hadn't expected to see Meg there, not understanding what they wanted her for or why she wasn't in the dungeon. As far as he could tell she hadn't been harmed, but he was helpless to save her and he couldn't even reassure her she would be fine. He had been able to make eye contact with her though, but the look of despair she'd given him in return made him sad to the bone.

'Let me out of here!' John shouted upwards to the grate, jaw still aching. 'I'll swing for you all!'

'You'll swing soon enough, wolfshead!' One of the guards shouted back, a bucket of slop following his words.

John spluttered and coughed, wiping the disgusting smelling liquid from his eyes. Sitting on the floor, his back against the damp wall, he looked around him.

The prison was full. John could normally recognise some of the scoundrels and those down on their luck who'd been brought here, but he was too agitated about Meg to pay anyone close attention. While he was glad she wasn't being subjected to this pestilent Hell, he couldn't help but think that, if she was in here with him, at least she wouldn't be upstairs, suffering under the hands – or worse – of the sheriff.

He looked up again at the grate and hoped Robin and the others were formulating a plan to get them both free. Damn his own thick skull for being so impulsive, he cursed.

Suddenly, a face appeared above the criss-crossed iron, silhouetted by flickering torchlight. It was Gisburne. He was looking straight down at John. Their eyes met for what seemed like an eternity. Then the man was gone.

Momentarily bemused by the peculiar and silent exchange, John's thoughts of Gisburne were knocked from him by a wiry, half-naked old man shuffling towards him while cradling a rat in his bony hands.

'Feet first…'

'Are you still in here?' John asked incredulously, having met this prisoner before on one of his very first visits to the gaol.

'It's the only way, isn't it, Arthur?'

John slumped against the wall, watching the old man and his rat disappear back into a gloomy corner. He glanced back up to the grate, but no more familiar and unnerving faces were staring back at him.

***

While John's current lodgings were dark and depressing, Meg's were bright and airy. The sun shone into her chambers, but it wasn't enough to lighten her thoughts. She didn't want to sit on the large bed, instead she chose to stand and stare out of the high window across the fields to distant Wickham.

Meg had feared losing John almost from the moment she'd fallen in love with him. She'd often have nightmares of him locked up in some goal somewhere, injured, sentenced to death, or lying injured in Sherwood; in pain and dying. She'd stay awake for hours some nights wondering if he'd ever come back. When he asked her to marry him and she'd said yes without even hesitating, those fears were still prevalent. Never had she imagined that she'd be a prisoner of the sheriff herself, sentenced to a living death by being the wife of a cold, unfeeling knight.

Meg turned away from the window and looked at the bed in disgust. She'd rather sleep on the wooden flooring. Looking at the door, she wondered if it was still locked.

Trying the handle, she wasn't surprised when it wouldn't budge. As she let go, a slight sound made her freeze to the spot.

Someone was there, on the other side of the door, lurking in the corridor. Meg placed a palm against the cool wood, then took it away almost immediately and retreated back into the centre of the room.

***

Gisburne was close to knocking on Meg's door but thought better of it. He felt unnerved that he'd even considered the act of politeness in the first place.

Seeing John Little staring back up at him from that vile hellhole had sparked some curiosity in him; what would a villager like Meg see in a disgusting, unkempt wolfshead? Why would she be horrified at the idea of marrying into a knighthood, to better herself? She'd automatically become Lady Gisburne and would have access to riches and wealth she could have only dreamed about before.

Marrying a serf was naturally quite unpalatable, Gisburne felt, but perhaps it *was* time he found a woman for himself. He wasn't getting any younger and his time in Normandy had given him a new perspective on life. He knew now that living under the cutting barbs of de Rainault's reign wasn't the be all and end all. There was more to life. He just had to take a leap of faith.

Even though this wedding was merely a ploy to capture Robin Hood and the other outlaws, Gisburne found himself wondering what might happen if he went through with the ceremony and he really *did* marry Meg?

CHAPTER 8

'You don't seem to be drinking, boy. Is there's something wrong with my ale?'

Much looked up through a foggy haze, but he couldn't work out if his vision were blurred because of the smoky fire or because he'd consumed a couple of tankards of whatever it was Will had suggested he'd drink.

The landlord was huge: taller and wider even than Little John, with a beard far bushier. His arms were folded over a dirty leather apron, his rotund belly jutting out from under his elbows. One of his eyes appeared to be half-closed, but the other was wide and all-seeing.

'I...' Much tried to begin but sighed in that way that indicated his tongue had decided not to co-operate with the rest of his mouth.

'He's not used to such a fine brew!' Will slapped Much hard between the shoulder blades, causing the younger man to groan – not from the blow but from the ale that was sloshing around in his belly and dispersing into his veins. 'I'll take another!'

Passing Will a large clay bottle, the landlord clunked it down on the table near to where Much's head was resting. He looked suspiciously at the coins Will tossed his way. 'You've over-paid there, my friend,' he said as he slid the coins into his apron anyway.

Will, almost as sober as the moment he stepped through the door to the Old Cross Inn, grabbed the landlord's bulging forearm, stopping him from walking away. 'Wait.'

The landlord glared at Will's hand. 'You'd best remove that.'

Scarlet's grip tightened. He didn't need ale to boost his courage. 'The rest of the coin was for information not the ale.'

'I've got none for you.'

'You don't know what we need to know yet.'

'You're strangers here, the pair of you.' The landlord looked from Will to Much, and back again. 'Your young companion clearly isn't used to his drink, but you…you've downed more than enough to knock out a horse.'

Will let go his grip. 'We're looking for someone.'

The landlord waived a hand casually. 'There's a few to choose from in here. Anyone in particular?'

'Yes.'

'Well I've not seen them.' The landlord stepped back. 'Now if you don't mind, I have other customers to see to.'

'Bethla.'

The landlord tensed for a split second. 'I don't know anyone called Bethla.'

'By the look on your face, you know exactly who I'm talking about.' Will said, 'young-ish woman, about so tall.'

'I run a respectable tavern…'

Will snorted a laugh and raised his tankard. 'Yeah, right!'

'I run a respectable tavern and I won't have mention of that… that woman in here.'

'So you *do* know her?'

The landlord looked furtive and sat himself down opposite Will. 'She causes me trouble.'

Will smiled. 'A big man like you? Scared of her?'

'I'm not scared of her. She just needs to know her place, that's all.'

'And what trouble does she cause, exactly, that you and your patrons can't deal with?'

'She…' The landlord broke off and sneered at the outlaws. 'You're mocking me. I know your game.'

'We can help you.' Will's gravelled voice cut through the noisy throng. 'We've been sent to help.'

The landlord was suspicious, but he was intrigued. Bethla was a burden to him – to them all. 'Help? How?'

'We can take her away for you.'

'How will you find her?' The landlord leaned in. 'She has ways of making herself disappear. Like a…'

Will concluded the big man wasn't brave enough to finish his own sentence. 'Like a witch?'

The single eye widened at the mention. 'Keep your voice down, stranger. You'll summon her.'

'We can deal with her.'

'How?'

'Leave that to us.'

'To you? A drunk boy and a...'

'A what?' Will's patience was running out. 'Do you want our help or not?'

The landlord sat back on the stool. 'Alright.'

'That's more like it.' Will placed his tankard on the table, 'Now, where can we find her?'

***

Will crept to the rear of the tavern, leaving a sleeping Much propped up outside. Two flagons weren't enough to keep him unconscious for long but he'd probably wake up with a sore head.

No doubt Robin will have a go at me for allowing Much to get drunk. Now... where is this woman everyone is so terrified of?

Before him, the field sloped downwards for an acre or two, to a line of trees and a series of small ramshackle buildings, one of which had a curl of smoke coming from a broken chimney stack.

Shirebrook wasn't a large town and it had been easy enough to find the general location of where Bethla had been seen.

The outlaws had heard stories of a woman from Chesterfield being accused of witchcraft and similar tales sprouting up in Shirebrook. There had also been rumours of a girl being abducted from her family home also in Chesterfield.

There were many similar stories that reached Robin's ears all the time, runaways and outcasts, and as much as he'd have liked to, he simply couldn't save them all. But after Herne had arrived, not long after Meg's forthcoming wedding had been announced, and shown him a vision of the 'witch of Shirebrook who is not as she seems', Robin decided to send Will and Much to find out the truth about this woman. It was too much of a co-incidence that the Lord of the Trees had directed them to Shirebrook at that time too ignore his prophecy.

Will, however, was unconvinced of the connection. 'Fine time to be going off rescuing would-be witches when we should be in Nottingham,' he mumbled as he edged nearer a group of ramshackle buildings at the far side of the town. 'Robin might think the woman could be useful to us, but I can't see how any sort of magic's gonna help. It only ever causes trouble.'

Will was still grumbling to himself about it now as he reached a group of rundown huts behind the houses. Unsheathing his sword, he investigated the area before entering the only hut to have smoke escaping from it.

As he walked through the door of the semi roofless structure, that had walls that would topple with the next strong gust of wind by looking at them, a few rats scurried away from him. The stench of the place was pungent. Scarlet screwed up his nose as he stepped further inside, expecting to see a few animal corpses were rotting in the corners.

Will had seen many sights over the years, which would shock and sicken the average person, but as he reached the back of the building, what he saw took his breath away.

There, chained to a wall, with an allowance of maybe a yard to move around, was a woman, no older than Much, covered in sores and dirt. In fact, Will had to stare at her for a few moments to see if she really was a woman, she looked that pitiful. The stink of the place made him wretch; it wasn't a rotting rat or two, it was the shackled girl.

'Bloody 'ell,' Will murmured and crouched down to her level where she was huddled against the crumbling wall. She looked at him, terrified, and tried to press herself against the wall even more. The chain at her left ankle cut deep into her flesh. 'Who did this to you?'

She looked over his shoulder.

'Them up there? The villagers?'

The woman nodded.

'You're Bethla?'

She nodded again.

'I'm Will Scarlet. I'm not from the village. I'm from Sherwood.' He went to move forward; reaching out a hand, but she cowered back. 'It's alright, I'm here to help you.'

What's wrong with the people of Shirebrook that they are willing to treat someone like this? He looked at the fire burning in the hearth. At least someone had taken pity on her. 'I'm going to get you away from here.'

'W-why?' she croaked.

'They think you're a witch, don't they?'

Bethla shrugged a yes. 'So they keep me here.'

'What for?'

'They think I'll curse them if they kill me.'

'So chaining you up is their solution?'

'I'd rather be dead.'

'Will you let me help you?'

Bethla looked at the stranger through exhausted eyes. He'd shown her more kindness in the few moments he'd been here than for all the time she'd been in Shirebrook. 'What did you say your name was?'

39

'Will.'

'Can you really get me away from here, Will?'

'I can!' Will bent to examine Bethla's chained ankles and wrists. He'd need to be gentle to get the manacles off. He wondered if someone in the tavern had keys, but he didn't want to bring them down here as he couldn't trust himself not to lash out at them. So he opted for using a carefully placed stone, patience and brute force – and, with more than a few apologies to her for the pain he caused – the manacles finally fell away from her sore flesh. 'Can you walk?'

Bethla nodded.

As she smiled at Will, he noticed her grey eyes, surrounded by matted blonde hair and dirt-caked skin. They were beautiful and full of gratitude.

Under there, he mused, *she must look very pretty.*

CHAPTER 9

Although there was some benefit in freeing John from the dungeon before the ceremony, Robin was insistent that he should stay where he was for the time being.

'If he is found to be missing from the gaol, then the sheriff will know we're in the castle,' Robin said.

'John won't be happy if he's in there for too long,' said Tuck.

'Are you absolutely sure we can stay hidden for a day and half in the castle without being recognised?' Marion had tucked her voluminous locks under a blue headscarf and changed into a pinafore dress. Her sword, hidden in the dress' lining, felt cumbersome.

Robin had used charcoal to dye his hair black. He hoped it wouldn't rain over the next few days. Even though it was in a ponytail and under a hat, he wouldn't fool anyone if the charcoal began to run out of his blonde locks. Marion had laughed at him when he'd appeared in his new guise, wearing an outfit of Lincoln green, with two small wooden cages slung over his shoulder and a collection of small nooses at his belt.

'And who exactly are you meant to be?' she asked through giggles.

'I'm George a' Green, pinder of Wakefield, ma'am.' Robin gave a theatrical bow. 'Here to serve and take from out of sight those scurrying animals that might otherwise disturb the nuptials of good Sir Guy and his bride to be.'

'It'll take more than a couple of cages to get rid of the rats in Nottingham,' said Tuck.

'I know,' Robin grinned.

'How do you think Meg is doing?' wondered Marion.

'I don't think they would have put her in the dungeon,' Robin replied.

'No?'

'She's marrying nobility. Even if Gisburne is about as noble as louse. They'll keep her out of harms' way. And if John is there, too, they must know of his relationship with her – so they wouldn't put them together.'

'But why Meg?'

'Probably because they know she's a good way of getting to us. And of course because she's a commoner,' Tuck said. 'If she were a Lady then the marriage would involve land and chattels and permissions of fathers and what not. By them taking from the people, none of that is an issue.'

'But Meg…poor girl,' said Marion.

'Poor John, too,' added Robin, 'knowing that his beloved will soon be another man's property.'

'Property…' Marion sneered. 'The quicker that gets changed the better. I'm no one's property and never will be!'

Robin looked a little crestfallen, but he knew what she meant. Even if one day she would marry him – and by Herne's goodness he hoped she would – he would never burden her with the pressures of being a goodly wife who knew her place. He would treat her equally, as all of them did already in Sherwood. He smiled at the image of someone trying to tell Marion what to do.

***

Gisburne strode up to the head gaoler, who stood to attention, pushing his half-eaten meal from Sir Guy's sight.

'Have you moved the prisoner as I instructed?'

'Yes, my Lord,' the gaoler replied. 'He's down below.'

Gisburne nodded in acknowledgement and followed the man into a darker part of the dungeon, through narrow corridors, ducking where necessary and squinting to find his way.

In a cell just six yards square – with a grate in one wall that brought in the stench the moat and the contents of emptied chamber pots, and a single table and chair – Little John was manacled to the floor. He looked away as Gisburne entered and seated himself at the table.

'This area is used for interrogation mainly.'

'You already know everything about us,' John replied. 'What else do you want from me?'

'There is one thing that I do not understand.' Gisburne's blonde hair glowed in the light of the torches that were dotted around the walls. He waved the gaoler away and waited until the clanking of keys faded from earshot. 'Meg.'

'What have you done to her?' growled John, lunging at Gisburne. His chains held him back. It was probably why Gisburne appeared so calm; he knew John couldn't reach him to break his neck.

'I've not done anything to her. Yet.'

'You harm even a hair on her head and—'

'Yes. I've no doubt what you would like to do, but soon she and I will be married and you will never see her again.'

The anger John had felt when he'd seen Meg captured and taken from him was one thing but what Gisburne had just calmly announced was altogether something different. Worse than a blow to the guts with his own quarterstaff.

'I'll flay you alive, Gisburne!' John roared and launched himself towards the table again but this time with such force that Gisburne tensed, genuinely fearful for that moment that this outlaw giant could bring the very walls down around them. But when John stumbled back and fell to the ground, Gisburne stood; his self-assuredness had returned. In fact, standing over John now gave him a sense of dominance that even the sheriff rarely achieved.

He looked down at the panting man. 'Time is coming to an end for you, wolfshead. For all of you.'

'What's Meg to you?' John breathed, the iron pulling at his skin. 'Why her?'

'Why not?'

'Then what is it you want to ask me? You never been with a woman before?' John didn't think the jibe was anywhere near low enough but was too angry to think of anything worse.

Gisburne's reply took John by surprise. 'I don't understand what she would see in you.'

'More than what she'd see in a foppish fool like you.'

'How strange. She said almost the same thing herself.'

Good for you, lass. 'She's locked up here somewhere?'

'Somewhere.' Gisburne looked thoughtful. 'What would you do to save her?'

'From marrying you?'

'My Lord Sheriff has given her two options. Marry me or hang.'

'I know what I'd prefer,' murmured John.

'This is no light matter, wolfshead,' responded Gisburne. 'Her life depended on her response.'

John tensed. 'Depended? She's given you a response?'

Gisburne nodded. 'She opted to hang.'

The outlaw leant back against the wall. 'Oh, my Meg…' he breathed.

'So that leaves me with something of a dilemma.'

'You?'

'I have no great desire to watch the woman be executed. I have better things to do. But I have been ordered by my Lord Sheriff to carry it out.' Gisburne crouched down to John's level, still careful to maintain his distance. 'But if I could offer something better for him to watch in her place...'

'Like what?'

'You could save her.'

'How? By giving myself up in her place? By admitting I'm an outlaw?'

'My Lord Sheriff doesn't need your confession. The fact that you are an outlaw is not in doubt.' Gisburne stood, his legs aching from a wound he suffered in Normandy. 'I could arrange for your pardon, and you and Meg can go free and live the rest of your pathetic lives in a hole somewhere for all I care.'

'You don't have the power to arrange that. You're just the sheriff's lacky.'

'What I am to the sheriff is not your business.'

John snorted derisively. 'We're outlaws and you're his pet. That's well-known, too.'

Gisburne clenched his fists and glared at John.

He was tired of being the butt of the de Rainault's jokes. No one respected him here. Normandy had shown him much more, far more than he had even imagined. His day would come.

'Give up Robin Hood, betray him so he'll hang in Meg's place, and your wench will live. If you do not, Meg will hang the day after tomorrow.'

***

When the single bird call sounded, Will recognised it as Nasir signalling to say it was safe for them to make their way towards the outlaw's camp. As they moved forward, Nasir jumped down from a thick tree branch where he'd been on watch and accompanied Will and his entourage the last few yards.

Will tried not to chuckle when he saw what Robin was wearing as he introduced everyone to Bethla.

The young woman was clearly nervous. Sensing her anxiety, Marion came forward to greet her.

'Come and sit by the fire. You look hungry. I hope Will has been looking after you,' Marion said, noticing Scarlet's attentiveness to their guest. 'Let's get you something to eat before it gets too dark.'

Bethla stared into her lap. Marion was about to reassure her when Much suddenly staggered into the camp.

Marion gasped. 'Much! What's happened to you? Are you hurt badly?'

Will laughed. 'Hurt? All he's hurt is his arm from too much drinking!'

Much groaned as he slumped next to Robin. 'Oh, my head…'

'You got him drunk, Will?' admonished Robin. 'What were you thinking?'

'He's alright! He's only 'ad a couple of flagons,' Will shrugged. 'Big flagons, mind…'

'Will!' Marion slapped Scarlet in mock disgust. 'You are a bad influence.'

'We all forget he's not a boy anymore! Puts hairs on his chest!' Will grabbed a leg of roasted meat and was about to bite into it when he paused, offering it to Bethla instead. 'Want it?'

Bethla shook her head, not looking up.

'Bethla, it's fine. You're among friends now. We will look after you,' soothed Robin. 'Can you tell us what happened to you?'

No response came so Marion ladled some of Tuck's broth into a bowl for her. Bethla looked at it, sniffed it and shook her head.

'She's got good taste!' Will laughed.

'There's nothing wrong with my cooking!' Tuck rolled his eyes but kept his usual good humour.

Marion winked at Robin as she saw Bethla give a vague smile. 'It may smell funny, but it tastes good.'

Bethla wasn't convinced. She leaned to the fire and peered into the big pot with its contents simmering away. Without saying anything she stood and scanned the woodland behind them.

'Are you alright?' asked Robin, concerned.

Bethla, in silence, moved into the dark. They all looked nervously at each other and Will went to follow her. Robin raised a hand.

'Wait a moment, Will.'

Bethla returned with a handful of thin green stalks, shredded them between her fingers and dropped them in the pot. Grabbing the ladle, she stirred the broth around then tasted it a couple of times. She nodded to herself and offered the ladle to Marion.

'It's good now.'

Marion took a sip and smiled. It *was* good. Tuck was a wonderful cook – they loved his food and loved teasing him – but Bethla's ingredient gave it a spicy touch.

'What did you add?'

'Spignel,' Bethla replied. 'It's not too common here.'

'Lucky you found some then,' said Will, trying the broth for himself. 'That's tasty.'

Robin sat next to Bethla. 'We think you might be able to help us.'

'Help? I don't think I can.'

'You have a reputation that I don't think has reached Nottingham yet.'

'What do you mean by reputation?' Bethla looked around at Robin and the others.

Marion put a hand on Bethla's forearm. 'We know you have been accused of witchcraft.'

'If that was so, and if I am a witch, you have all just been poisoned.'

'But you 'ad some yourself,' pointed out Will.

'Perhaps I've been eating that herb for some time and have become accustomed to its effects.'

'Oh.' Will dropped the ladle to the ground.

Bethla smiled. 'But I am in a strange land. Poisoning you would leave me here all alone.'

'I don't think you'd wish us any harm, Bethla,' said Marion.

'You're very kind to get me away from that place. I would like to repay you.' Bethla stood and walked around the fire, her anxiety easing by every moment. 'I am not a witch but yes, I have been accused of such.'

'Why?' asked Much.

'Because I know the land, the herbs,' she continued, nodding to the pot. 'I heal people. Or I try to.'

Robin understood. 'And when you couldn't help someone, they turned on you?'

'Yes. One of the village daughters. She was with child and I was made to help because she had pains in her belly. The child was born…not alive. I was blamed for its death and they kept me prisoner as punishment.'

Robin shook his head. 'That's terrible.'

'I didn't kill the child!' Bethla blurted, too used to defending herself against those who didn't believe. 'I didn't!'

'Why would you?' Marion said, motioning for Bethla to retake her seat. 'We believe you.'

'You're free of them now,' said Will. 'There's no one here to blame you. You should trust us.'

'We have two friends in great peril,' Robin said then. 'We want you to help us save them.'

Bethla looked confused, her breathing shallow. 'But I don't understand. What help can I give you?'

'You've already shown us you can give a kick to a pot of soup,' said Robin.

'How would you like to do the same to a whole banquet?' asked Marion.

'Except this time the kick will be to put everyone to sleep,' added Robin.

CHAPTER 10

Flynn sat by Jonas's side in the guard house, watching as the two monks Abbot Hugo had commandeered from the abbey tended to the captain's wounds.

While he and Jonas had not always seen eye to eye, Flynn felt sorry for him. The man was in agony and there was no one else to show even a morsel of concern.

A muttering from the monks bent over Jonas caused their patient to catch his breath sharply. Flynn looked at the captain's pale face as the clerics mumbled prayers over his stricken body. It was clear they couldn't save him.

One of the monks gestured for Flynn to join him on the other side of the small room. 'I'm sad to say he will not see sunrise. May the Lord protect his soul.'

'I understand,' Flynn replied. He had been in the sheriff's employ for some time now, and although he'd seen plenty of wounded men, he'd never witnessed anything so severe. He hoped for Jonas' sake that the end wasn't far away.

Sitting back by the dying man's side, Flynn was surprised when Jonas slowly raised a shaking hand and moved his lips.

Leaning in close, keeping his gaze away from the coil of guts the monks had yet to cover up, Flynn spoke gently, 'Save your strength, Jonas.'

But Jonas persisted, trying to mouth something to his colleague.

Flynn put his ear near. 'What is it?'

'S… s-sun.'

'Water, quickly. He is trying to tell me something.'

A monk squeezed a rag across Jonas' cracked and dry lips, before dipping some moisture down his throat. 'Slowly,' the monk soothed as Jonas tried to swallow in gulps.

'What are you trying to say?' Flynn asked.

'S-s-sun... search th...'

Flynn frowned. 'I don't understand'

'It is normal for the dying to see things we cannot,' said the monk.

'No, he wants us to look somewhere.' Flynn followed the weak gesturing of Jonas' fingers. They were waving towards his bloodied chainmail and tunic, piled in a heap on the floor. 'Your clothes?'

Jonas blinked his eyes in confirmation.

'What am I looking for?'

'Su-sun.'

Flynn still didn't understand but went over the clothes anyway and picked them over for something unusual. Soon, under the mail, he found a small piece of cloth. Pulling it free, Flynn turned it over in his hands as he walked back to Jonas.

'Is this it?'

Jonas painfully and imperceptibly nodded. 'Sun.'

Flynn looked at the emblem of a sun embossed in gold on one side. The nearby monk gasped and stepped back as soon as he caught sight of it, crossing himself twice and grabbing his rosaries. It was as if the piece of cloth was soaked in evil, not just in Jonas' blood.

'This is yours? What is it?' Flynn had never seen anything like it.

'Not... m-mine.'

'Whose then?'

'G... g...'

'Jonas, why is this important? Whose is it?'

Keep... it... safe,' Jonas wheezed, the simple act of speaking sending unalloyed pain through his body. 'Use...'

'Use? Use it for what?'

'B-bargain.'

Flynn nodded. He was beginning to see what Jonas meant. 'Does who this belongs to know you have it?'

Jonas smiled.

'He needs to rest, my Lord,' the monk said, unnerved by the scrap of cloth. 'That needs to be burnt with the rest of his clothes.'

'In a moment,' Flynn was well aware that Jonas needed to rest, but this intrigued him and it was obviously vital to Jonas that he took the cloth. 'Who does this belong to? Jonas? Jonas!'

Flynn placed a hand on Jonas's shoulder but the man had become limp and seemed to sink into the hard cot.

'He is gone,' the other monk said.

'Jonas! *Who* does this belong to?'

It was too late. Flynn was talking to a dead man. Stepping back, he motioned for the monk to cover Jonas' body with the blood-soaked sheet. This second monk had also seen the scrap of cloth but appeared far less disturbed by its presence.

'Do you know what this is?' Flynn asked him.

The monk tilted his head and retreated from Jonas' lifeless form. 'I wish no conversation about it.'

'Somebody must know...' Flynn looked at it again then stared at the shrouded Jonas. 'But you've taken that information with you, haven't you?'

Flynn left the room, the cloth tight in his grip.

***

Little John, still manacled in the large cell, was struggling to make sense of Gisburne's offer. There was cruelty and then there was bitter spitefulness. Gisburne had both in equal measure.

John sighed. He knew that, even if he agreed to Gisburne's offer to swap hanging Meg for betraying Robin, so he was hanged instead, there was still a chance Gisburne would double cross him. Then all the outlaws might hang— along with Meg.

There was a chance however, albeit slim, that Gisburne would act with some element of honour, and keep his word. A thought which sent John's head spinning back to the original dilemma.

Robin dies or Meg dies.

The options couldn't be any simpler.

It was making the choice that was impossible.

John started to work the problem through his head all over again. If he agreed, and handed Robin to Gisburne, Robin might escape and John and Meg would be okay, because they'd already have been freed. On the other hand, if he refused, Meg would have no chance of rescue. She would hang and John would be left with the guilt for the remainder of his life. Plus, if he did betray Robin and the Hooded Man couldn't escape, then – although John would be a free man, pardoned, living the rest of his life with the woman he loved – he'd always have to live with the knowledge that he was responsible for the death of his friend.

He knew what Robin would say. *She's the love of your life, John. You deserve to spend it with her.*

And Meg? *I couldn't live with the knowledge that you sacrificed your friend to be with me.*

49

John sank back against the hard floor with a groan, knowing no matter how long he wrestled with the problem, he'd never come up with the right answer.

***

The next morning, the sheriff went to visit the kitchens. His presence threw the servants into a panic as he strode in, demanding to see the boar that had brought one of his men to an untimely end.

Gisburne, hard on his master's heels, eyed the bustle with great interest. Flynn and the huntsmen had caught enough game to let the wedding feast last for a whole week, let alone a day. Gisburne was quietly impressed.

'If that imbecile Jonas hadn't impaled himself on a pig's tusks, we could have had far more to eat for your cherished ceremony,' de Rainault spat. 'But that said, there's more food here than your betrothed has probably seen in her entire life, eh, Gisburne?'

'Yes, my Lord.'

Gisburne knew the sheriff wasn't out to impress anyone with the amount of preparation that was going on around them, nor was he going to such lengths to show uncharacteristic generosity to the peasants. Neither was it to soften the blow to Gisburne himself for the mock wedding. No, this was de Rainault enjoying taking advantage of the fact that Hugo was paying for the wedding.

So be it, thought Gisburne. He hadn't faced the prospect of such a fine feast since before his time in Normandy, and the varied meats (goose, beef and lamb as well as the hunted boar) would sit well in his stomach, washed down by the wine he'd need to go through with the ridiculous plan. Although, he knew he couldn't enjoy himself too much on the feast: if Robin Hood and his men would be in attendance, then he'd need his wits about him to ensure the wolfsheads' successful capture.

Picking up an apple, the sheriff gave it a sniff, rubbed it on his tunic and took a bite. Seconds later, the arrival of a filthy-looking wretch at his ankles made the previously sweet fruit taste sour.

'What do you want?' De Rainault threw the apple to the ground as he chewed on the bitter pulp.

The young boy didn't dare look his masters in the eye.

'Well? Speak, boy!' Gisburne snapped.

'It's about Rintoul, my Lords.'

'Rintoul?' The sheriff looked at Gisburne, who shrugged.

'The cook, my Lords.'

'What about him?' asked the sheriff.

50

'He's been taken to his bed,' the boy replied.

'This is no time to sleep. Get him back here at once,' Gisburne demanded.

'He's not well, my Lords.'

'Not well?' The sheriff raised an eyebrow. 'What's wrong with him?'

'It was something he ate,' said the boy.

'Why am I surrounded by incompetents?' snapped the sheriff as he struck the unfortunate boy across the head.

'How are we going to get all of this ready by tomorrow? It's not possible,' declared Gisburne.

'You're not getting out of if that easy,' snarled de Rainault. 'Feast or no, you're still getting married, Gisburne. Boy, find someone else to replace this Rintoul.'

The young lad nodded and dashed into the gloom.

'You're in charge of the servants, Gisburne. I hope you didn't poison the cook yourself.'

'Of course not, my Lord.'

They were about to depart the kitchens when they heard a sudden commotion coming from near the large ovens. Investigating, Gisburne saw a woman holding counsel with a knife, shouting to the other servants that preparing a goose in that way would most likely ruin the entire feast.

'You'll all be hanged, you idiots!' she yelled, 'Take it out and throw it away.'

A skewer appeared amidst the shouting and one of the servants made to withdraw the goose from its rack.

'Wait!' Gisburne commanded. 'You will not waste your masters' food.' He turned to the woman. 'Who are you to give such orders?'

'What's going on, Gisburne?' asked the sheriff as he came up behind Sir Guy.

'This woman here… She considers your brother's generosity to be such that she wishes to throw good food away.'

'Is that so?' The sheriff looked her up and down. Her grey eyes held a keen interest in what was going on around her, her thick blonde hair tied in a neat plait behind her head. The sheriff saw her hands were clean, nails devoid of grime. 'You claim you can cook do you?'

'I do indeed, my Lord Sheriff.'

'How long have you been here?'

'Not long.'

'Do you recognise her, Gisburne?'

Gisburne shook his head, 'She must have been brought in with the last admission of servants, my Lord.' He turned to the woman, 'What's your name?'

51

'Bethla.'

'Well, Bethla,' de Rainault's shrewd gaze assessed her for a second, 'if you can cook, and if you can do so without killing anybody, a cooks place has become available here.'

'Available, my Lord?'

'It seems Gisburne here appointed a cook who can't stomach his own receipt. You are charged to take over and ensure the wedding banquet is ready for the morning.'

'But...' Bethla frowned, feigning concern at her own abilities.

'If you poison anybody or give anyone rotten guts, you'll be hanged by noon tomorrow.'

'I understand, my Lord Sheriff,' Bethla responded with a curtsey.

As Gisburne and de Rainault moved off, she gave a sly wink to Much, who, hidden in the shadows, had kept his head down while busily kneading bread.

CHAPTER 11

The hawk spun and dived, catching the breeze on its soft feathers, using the updraft to soar over the heads of the watching crowd. The bell on its left leg tintinnabulated with its graceful movements.

The bird landed neatly and elegantly on the outstretched arm of the falconer, his thick leather sleeve keeping the hawk's needle-sharp claws at bay. The crowd cheered and clapped as they falconer bowed and gave the hawk a morsel of mouse before re-hooding it.

The show over, the crowd dispersed across the grounds of Nottingham castle.

Will Scarlet, a grubby bandage over one eye, leaning on a crutch, hobbled over to Robin, still dressed as a pinder.

'She's in and the sheriff has given her the job of head cook,' he whispered, keeping his voice as low as possible.

Robin nodded and smiled nonchalantly at a woman passing by who looked with horror at the rat in one of his cages. 'And Much?'

'He's with her. Hopefully, they won't recognise him. He said that Gisburne and the sheriff probably won't go back to the kitchens so they should be safe down there.'

'Where's Tuck?' Will asked.

***

In a deep part of Sherwood, the gentle rhythmic tapping of the pots suspended from either side of the little caravan heralded its ever-onwards motion through the thick woods towards the outskirts of Nottingham.

It was a dull looking contraption; faded after years of exposure to the

English elements. Its curved roof was green and black with either mould or dirt or both, the true colour beneath long since obscured.

The man, a minister, had been summoned by the Lord High Sheriff of Nottingham to perform the marriage service of Sir Guy of Gisburne to Meg of Wickham and, while it was not his place to question such a summons (certainly when he was being very well-paid for the task), he had concluded that trouble lay ahead.

Although he travelled alone, Father Apollinari felt secure in the protection of his belief – not to mention the dagger which nestled against his thigh and the longbow by his side. He never carried gold with him, just the simple wooden objects of his faith, so was rarely a target for unscrupulous highwaymen and other nefarious robbers.

Father Apollinari, however, hadn't accounted for Friar Tuck.

'How goes the day?' Tuck asked as he stepped into the track, blocking Apollinari's way. He held a quarterstaff, its tip resting on the ground, his other hand hooked into his belt.

Apollinari pulled up on the reigns, bringing his horse to a stop. He squinted over the beast's back at the interruption, tugging at his long beard in concern.

'Are you lost, my son?' he asked, a lilt betraying his Sardinian roots.

'I was just wondering the same thing about your good self,' replied Tuck. 'It's a beautiful day but these roads to Nottingham can be treacherous.'

'Have no fear for my safety, my son,' Apollinari replied, indicating the longbow on the narrow wooden seat next to him.

'Ah,' Tuck nodded. 'You expect trouble?'

'One should always be prepared, Brother—?'

'Tuck.'

'Brother Tuck, would you like to accompany me?' Apollinari motioned for the friar to sit next to him. 'I would hate to think that you are at risk yourself of attack from the blaggards who roam these woods.'

'All have souls to save, Father—?'

'Apollinari.'

'Do you know of any blaggards around these parts, then?' Tuck asked as he clambered, with a few huffs and puffs, up onto the wagon.

'I have travelled many lands and seen many things. I would be surprised if there aren't any.' Apollinari flicked the reigns. 'Walk on.'

The horse plodded onwards, its tail-swishing.

'I take it you're on your way to Nottingham for the ceremony?'

'Indeed. I am to marry the happy couple.'

Tuck kept Apollinari's attention, talking at length of Nottingham, speaking well of Gisburne and his bride. They travelled together through Sherwood, the sunlight flickering through the trees, flurries of birds overhead.

After a while, Apollinari said: 'I was led to believe that Sherwood was rife with outlaws. We seem to have been very fortunate so far.'

'Fortune has nothing to do with it, Father Apollinari.' Tuck smiled, crossing himself as Nasir emerged silently from the forest. He had a knife at the minister's throat in seconds.

Apollinari dived for his longbow, but Nasir was faster, throwing it out of the minister's reach. The churchman scrabbled for his dagger, but his hand found nothing but his belt.

Tuck grinned as he waved Apollinari's own dagger in his face.

'Why you... you... sacrilegious...'

'Outlaw?' Tuck finished. 'Nasir...'

As Tuck took the reins, Nasir grabbed Apollinari's arms, binding them behind his back before placing a muzzle over his mouth.

'In case you cry out,' Nasir said.

Despite putting up hearty resistance, Apollinari was, unceremoniously, bundled into the back of the wagon. He looked longingly at the longbow next to him, but his bonds were too tight to wriggle out of them. Up ahead, he saw the unlikely duo side by side, a Saracen and a fat friar, their trickery sharper than any weapon.

***

Gisburne stood outside Meg's door, his thoughts disturbed. He could hear her walking around, but were there tears, too? She didn't seem like the sort who would cry. *But who knows how women think!*

He considered announcing his presence first, but then flung the door open anyway. Meg was at the window, looking out across the fields. When she turned, he saw her eyes were red. Pushing her shoulders back, she stepped away from the window.

'It's customary to knock before entering a lady's room,' she said, trying her best to sound regal.

Gisburne was about to reply with a pithy comment about her level of social standing but thought better of it. 'I would speak with you.'

Over one arm Meg saw he held a gown. Coloured wine-red and pearl, it was simple but nevertheless ornate compared to what she was used to.

'I have nothing to say to you.'

'I suggest you think again.'

Meg looked at the gown. 'Do you expect me to wear that?'

'I do not expect you to wear what you usually consider to be acceptable.'

'Today is my wedding day,' she said.

'No. Tomorrow is our wedding day,' Gisburne corrected.

'My wedding day to John.' Tears tried to work their way to her eyes again but she held them back. 'It was meant to be today.'

'That is no longer your concern. He is to be forgotten.'

'Just like that? I marry you against my wishes and I have to forget about him?'

'That is what I came to tell you. You will forget him.' Gisburne put the dress on the bed. 'John Little is dead.'

'Dead?' Meg shook her head, hate for the man standing before her raging inside her. 'I don't believe you.'

'He was killed while trying to escape.'

'You're lying…' she said.

'He was attempting to rescue you. He got as far as the great hall. My men killed him.'

Meg staggered back. As she slumped to the bed her hand inadvertently touched the wedding dress. She looked at it, too angry to cry, but suddenly too exhausted to argue with Gisburne.

'They said he gave a good fight.'

Meg squeezed her eyes tight. That was her John; never giving up even when all seemed to be lost.

'Where is he now?'

'With…' He was about to answer that John's body had been dumped with all the other dead prisoners but thought better of it. 'In the guard room.'

'Can I see him?'

'That wouldn't be wise. He was badly injured. Perhaps you should remember him as he was.' Gisburne swallowed, finding the next few words distasteful. 'I'm sorry for your loss.'

'Are you?' Meg didn't believe him.

'I am.' He moved towards her. 'May I?' He gestured to the bed.

Without waiting for her consent he sat next to her. Meg's stomach churned as she felt his closeness. 'Do not touch me!'

Gisburne placed his hands on his knees. 'You will be happy here.'

'Will I?'

'I'll make sure you are. You are to be my wife and it is my duty to see you are well looked after.'

'And what's *my* duty to you?'

'I…'

Meg couldn't even bear to look at him. He *was* a fool. Her John, now there was a man. Strong, powerful, loving. This idiot wouldn't know what love was if it came with instructions. *How can I possibly say yes to him tomorrow? I'd rather hang.*

A knock came at the door. Meg was relieved at the interruption, hoping it would bring an end to their awkward conversation.

'Enter,' commanded Gisburne.

A woman came in, her head bowed, he hair tied under a scarf, she addressed Meg. 'M'lady, it is time for you to begin preparing for tomorrow.'

'A bit soon, isn't it?' Gisburne queried.

'There is much to get m'lady ready for, my Lord,' the woman responded.

'Well, erm, yes…of course. I'll take my leave of you,' Guy replied, flustered at the thought.

The woman waited the shadows for the door to close. She dashed to it to make sure Gisburne had gone, then turned to Meg.

'Marion!'

'Keep your voice down.' Marion hissed. 'Gisburne didn't see my face but he'll know my name!'

'I knew John wouldn't leave me here… It is true what Gisburne said?'

Marion led Meg to the bed and took her hand. 'Edward is here and he's checked the cells. John isn't in any of them.'

'So it is true… He *is* dead.' Meg gritted her teeth. 'Let's get out of here.'

'No.' Marion shook head. 'We're not leaving.'

'Why not? John's dead and I don't want to marry that fool.'

'Yes, John probably is dead. Other than the dungeon, there'd be nowhere else they'd keep him. They wouldn't risk putting him anywhere less secure.' Marion hurried to the window, struggling not to fall to pieces at the news of John's death in front of Meg. 'We're coming for you. Robin and Will are already in the grounds. We can't get you out until the feast is underway.'

'But the feast will only be after the ceremony. When I'm already be married to Gisburne!'

'We're delaying the minister. The sheriff won't want the food to go to waste while he's waiting for him to arrive. I just needed to tell you that you must play along.'

'With John dead what's the point?'

Marion grabbed her hands. 'I know what you're going through. That feeling of…of loss is indescribable, but we're all here to get you out. But for now please, try hard to be patient.'

Meg nodded, chewing on her bottom lip. 'I will, Marion.'

'Good. The sheriff will send ladies-in-waiting to you in the morning to help you get dressed.'

'Will you come back then?'

'No. It's too dangerous. When you get to the great hall, wait for our signal.'

'What will it be?'

'You'll know.' Marion stood and hugged Meg tight. 'It will be alright. Trust us.'

Then Marion was gone, out through the door and into the myriad of corridors, veins in the body of Nottingham castle.

Meg looked down at the red dress. John wouldn't want her to be here. He'd tell her to find a way to get out. And now that Marion was here with the others, the hope of rescue was back at the forefront of her mind.

CHAPTER 12

In a moment of unexpected benevolence on Gisburne's part, John had been freed from his manacles but kept in the large interrogation cell. As he sat at the table, chewing his way through a chunk of dry, stale bread, he could hear, through the grate, the sound of hammering and sawing outside.

He'd craned his neck earlier trying to peer through the grill but could only see vestiges of daylight. It didn't matter. He knew what the noise was. Gallows were being built for his beloved Meg.

He'd not wanted the bread, having no appetite in light of Gisburne's revelation that Meg had decided to hang rather than be married to the knight, but he wanted to keep his strength – just in case.

Today would have been their wedding day and the beginning of the rest of their lives. Instead, one of them was waiting to hang and the other might not see the outside of the castle's dungeon ever again.

He was angry with himself for storming off, for confronting Herne without talking to Robin first, and for endeavouring to rescue Meg alone. His friends were bound to try and rescue them, so they were now in peril because of him.

Throwing the rest of the crust across the cell, John kicked the chair back. It clattered against the floor, alerting a guard, who stared through the barred door John in contempt.

'Keep quiet in there, scum!'

John spun and bared his teeth at the man. He can't have been any older than Much but he clearly had more hate in him that Much would accumulate in a lifetime. 'Let me out of here.'

'You'll be out of here soon enough. Once the wench has married Sir Guy!'

John sneered. 'I'll break your scrawny neck...' he said and padded to the bars, then paused. What had the guard said?

'Your own neck will be broken on those gallows out there.'

'You said "when the wench has married Sir Guy"?'

'Yes. Are you too stupid to understand? Sir Guy is marrying her tomorrow.'

'I thought she was to be hanged?'

'That was only if she refused!'

'She's agreed to marry him?'

The guard had had enough of this conversation and left. John clasped his hands together and started pacing, the damp floor squelching under his boots. Gisburne had lied to him. Had tricked him! There was never going to be an exchange between of Meg for Robin!

John kicked out at the table. *I've been so stupid! The sheriff would never have allowed Robin's life to be spared for Meg's.*

John looked back at the barred door. There was still a chance to save her. All he had to do was get out of this prison.

***

Robin was sat on a bale of hay, threading string into little nooses. Will was some distance away still in his guise as a crippled beggar, sitting against the castle wall. Marion was browsing through the market stalls, not buying anything but keeping watch on everything that was going on around them. Edward, wearing a grey hood, was pretending to be entertained by a jester, who was dressed in a long coat of a multitude of colours beneath a mop of blonde curly hair.

Meanwhile, Much was in the kitchens with Bethla, preparing the feast for tomorrow while Tuck and Nasir were still in Sherwood, keeping a watch over the minister who should have arrived at Nottingham by now.

***

'And you've had no word from him?' De Rainault asked his brother.

'If he left his parish on time, then Father Apollinari would have been with us by now.' Hugo stepped out of the way as a team of servants began to shift long heavy tables into a line that extended out perpendicular to the head table in the great hall, where the sheriff regularly sat.

'I hope he's alright, my Lords,' said Gisburne.

'Do you, Gisburne? I sincerely doubt that. You would be overcome with delight if there was no one to marry you to the Wickham strumpet.' The sheriff barked an order to one of the servants to move all the tables a foot to the right. 'Perhaps, Hugo, you could marry them if your minister fails to appear. After all, this *was* your idea.'

'The sooner we can get Robin Hood and the other wolfsheads hanging from those gallows you're building out there the better,' Hugo said, fiddling with the heavy gold rings on his purple-gloved knuckles.

'We all feel the same, my Lord,' agreed Gisburne.

'I have to say though, brother, that this is a remarkably simple plan. Get all the outlaws in here then lock the doors. Too simple perhaps?'

'It can't fail,' Hugo snapped.

'And I'm sure you're more than happy that it's us that'll be locked in here with them and not you.' The sheriff raised an eyebrow. 'Why won't you be attending the wedding brother? Too scared of the possibility of an outbreak of violence?'

The abbot blustered, 'I told you Robert. I'm busy elsewhere!'

'Of course you are.' De Rainault sat back in his chair. 'Any sign of them yet, Gisburne?'

Guy shook his head. 'The upper ward is full of peasants, though.'

'See? You *are* popular,' the sheriff's grunted.

'…but Robin Hood does not seem to be among them. Yet.'

'Give it time. He'll turn up soon enough, swaggering in with that harlot Lady Marion on his arm, no doubt.' The sheriff's expression looked as if his wine had gone sour.

'If you will excuse me,' Gisburne said as he stood.

'Where are you off to?'

'I am going to see if Meg needs anything for tomorrow. She had a lady-in-waiting with her earlier.'

The sheriff glanced at Hugo, who smirked.

'Go on then,' Robert de Rainault said. 'Perish the thought that you leave your true-love for too long.'

Gisburne bowed once and left, leaving Hugo to turn his smirk into a fetid sneer. 'By God, Robert, if I didn't know any better, I'd say he was actually eager to see the woman. What in Heaven's name happened to him in Normandy?'

***

'What do you want?'

Gisburne didn't really expect Meg to be happy to see him, although she had no choice but to allow him entry to her chambers. What bothered him was that he wasn't quite sure why he'd gone to see her.

'Does everything suit your needs?'

Meg shook her head. 'No. It doesn't. But what does that matter?'

Gisburne moved to the window and looked out across the fields. 'Would you like a different view?'

'One that doesn't remind me I'm stuck here?'

'Perhaps if you overlooked the grounds of the castle itself? There are a great many people amassing. It could be quite a distraction for you.'

'Why?'

'Why what?'

'Why does it matter to you?'

Gisburne turned back to look at her. She was standing firm, still unwavering in her defiance. He had to admit that he admired that. Strength of character in a woman was a trait that appealed to him. It was a relief at least, that she wasn't some snivelling half-wit slip of a girl.

'I understand that this is not ideal, but you have to accept that this is your life from now on. I will look after you.'

'Look after me?' Meg threw her hands up in the air. 'It's not you who I want looking after me! It's—'

'John Little is *dead*. He won't be looking after anyone anymore!'

Meg held her forehead, willing tears not to flow again. She would not let this Norman fool see her cry. 'I don't need reminding.' Composing herself, Meg folded her arms. 'You're serious about this marriage? It's not some big joke?'

Just as she wouldn't let him see her vulnerable, Gisburne wouldn't let Meg know the real reason for the ceremony, to lure, capture and hang Robin Hood. Yet, unbeknown to the sheriff, he'd begun to develop his own reasons, for going through with it. Being married would affect his role as the de Rainault's deputy. He knew the sheriff wouldn't tolerate a woman around the place and he'd most likely send Gisburne off to another assignment, perhaps to govern a hamlet within the shire somewhere.

Gisburne could easily cope with replacing the sheriff's sharp tongue with that of a wife's. Free of the sheriff but lumbered with a bride – there were worse things in life.

'We will be married by this time tomorrow and there is nothing that your dead fiancé's friends can do about it.'

***

Dusk fell over Nottingham and the braziers gave some warmth to those settling down for the night in the grounds of the castle.

If Robin Hood was going to infiltrate the castle unseen, it was likely to happen between now and the morning. The sheriff had assigned disguised guards to stay hidden amongst the throng, watching the gates and the walls.

One such guard, dressed as a peasant, rubbed his hands together over a fire.

'It's going to be along night, eh?' said the figure on the ground next to him.

'Cold, too,' the guard answered, looking at the little cages the man was leaning on.

'George,' said Robin, introducing himself with a finger to his forehead. 'Pinder by trade. You?'

'Shepherd.'

Convinced his companion was lying, Robin concluded he was one of the sheriff's men. Anyone who spent hours out on the fields tending and herding sheep wouldn't complain about being cold so soon after the sun had begun to set.

And it's me you're to try and spot amongst the crowds. 'What brings you here? Enjoy a good wedding?'

The guard nodded.

'We don't often get nice reasons to celebrate, what with the sheriff telling us what to do all the time.'

Will, a few feet away and listening to this exchange, smiled under his bandages. Taunting a witless guard was reason enough itself to be here. He just wished John were with them. But perhaps the dungeon was a good place for him to be for the moment: the giant would have been spotted a mile off no matter what disguise he would have opted for.

Scarlet saw Marion nearby. She was walking slowly past a huddle of people. Some were sleeping, while others chatted happily, played checkers or skittles, or told stories. The forthcoming wedding made the mood bright in the grounds of the castle that night.

Dawdling until disguised guard had moved on, she sat next to "George", warming her hands over the brazier.

'Everything in place?' Robin asked without looking at her.

'Meg was told that John has been killed. I couldn't see him in the gaols. Do you think it's true?' Her voice was hoarse and low.

'I don't think they'd risk killing him. They know we're going to be here so killing him may bring our wrath down on them.' Robin looked over to Will who shook his head, agreeing that John probably hadn't seen his end.

'Or...' Marion wasn't so sure, '...the sheriff may use his death to gloat at the wedding?'

Robin considered that. 'Has Bethla tainted the food to be sent to the guard house yet?'

'Much will make sure she does.'

'They need to be asleep before the ceremony begins or we'll be in trouble.'

Marion nodded, adding, 'They're setting up the tables for the feast in the great hall at the moment.'

'The wedding will happen in there. Meanwhile, I suspect those,' Robin motioned to the gallows that had been erected, 'are for our benefit. Marion, do you think Meg will remain calm?'

Marion shrugged. 'I'm not so sure. If we can prove to her John isn't dead she'll play along, but right now, the fight has gone out of her.'

'The guard house first then, once Bethla has sent the food down,' Robin said.

Will feigned struggling to his feet, hobbling on a crutch toward Robin. He'd half-heard the end of the conversation and Robin reiterated it to him as quietly as he could.

'So it's agreed then?'

Will nodded. 'Guards at first light. But *before* that bloody cock crows.'

CHAPTER 13

'It's still the middle of the night!' cursed Robert de Rainault as one of his attendants lit the candles in his room. 'Get out! Get out!'

'Up, brother,' said Hugo as he ushered the servant out. 'It's your steward's big day.'

'Has the minister arrived yet?'

'He's been received by Flynn and is in the kitchens now.'

'Finally! But the kitchens? This is no time to eat! Shouldn't he be in the hall getting his incantations ready?'

'You'll burn in Hell for that, dear Robert.'

'At least you won't be alone down there then, *dear* Hugo. Why was he delayed?' The sheriff pulled himself up, rubbing his hands vigorously across his face.

'Flynn said something about a broken wheel.'

'Well he's here now. Is Gisburne still with us or did he hang himself from the gallows in the middle of the night?'

'He's being roused now.'

'More's the pity. Let's get on with it, then.'

The de Rainault brothers found Gisburne in his chambers arguing with two servants. They were trying to get him dressed in his finest tunic but it was a tight fit.

'I won't be able to breathe in this thing!'

'As long as you get the vows out, you can expire after if you wish,' the sheriff said. 'You'd better not do anything to jeopardise this, Gisburne.' Hugo added.

'I won't, my Lord,' Gisburne replied, stifling a yawn.

'I do hope you won't be doing that all through the blessing. Meg will think she's married a scopperloit.'

'I am tired, my Lord.'

'If you would be up all night polishing your helmet, then I'm not surprised,' replied the sheriff, picking up Gisburne's ceremonial headgear that positively gleamed in the candlelight.

Over a chair hung the finest chainmail Hugo had seen this side of Normandy. A sword in its scabbard leant against the window. 'Your finest armour?'

'If I didn't know you better, Gisburne, I'd say you were out to impress. I'm sure you implied you weren't interested in the woman.' The sheriff dropped the helmet back onto the chair.

'These are for your benefit, my Lord Sheriff.'

'*My* benefit? It's not me you're marrying.'

'No, my Lord, but with most of the shire in attendance, it seemed the correct thing to do.'

'How very thoughtful of you. Will you be this attentive to your wife?'

The two servants began to fuss around Sir Guy, lifting the heavy chainmail up over his head, getting his blonde hair caught in the process.

'You fools!' Gisburne snapped, wincing as the mail dropped onto his shoulders and the nearest servant timidly picked up a surcoat.

'How can you afford silk?' the sheriff asked. His own surcoat was of plain heavy cloth. 'Am I paying you too much?'

'It was given to me in Normandy.'

'Friends in high places, eh?' De Rainault felt the material between his fingers.

'Gerard De Rid- ouch!' Gisburne pushed one of the servants away, nursing his hand where he had hit it with the hilt of his sword. 'Just buckle it up and leave me be!'

As quickly as they could, the attendants ensured Gisburne's scabbard was hanging correctly, and hurried from the chamber.

'So this hag then, have you instructed her to know her place?'

'I'm not sure what you mean.'

'Oh come now, Gisburne, don't come across as all coy. How will you make sure the Wickham woman doesn't elevate herself?' The sheriff rolled his eyes, 'you may be making her a lady by marrying her, but you can't take the peasant out of a woman. You'll have to put her to work or she'll be unable to function.'

'Don't allow her any input into your business affairs,' added Hugo. 'And by God don't give her any land or chattels. We can't have women owning anything.'

Gisburne looked between the two brothers. Had they forgotten that this wedding was intended to be just a ruse? But if Gisburne did go through with it, he had to acknowledge that what they were saying was right. He couldn't have a wayward, hot-headed wife demanding all and sundry from him. It just wasn't the done thing.

He put his helmet under his arm and took a deep breath. 'My Lords…if you will…'

Hugo cut across Gisburne. 'Are your men ready, Robert?'

'I would hope so.' The sheriff slapped his deputy on the back. 'Come on, it's time to make an honest man of you, Gisburne. May God have mercy upon her soul.'

***

Much was carrying two large buckets of broth from the kitchens to the guard house when an old beggar stepped in his way.

'Much.' The beggar lifted the grubby bandages from one of his eyes.

'Will!' Much, looking furtively around them.

'We've not got a lot of time. Have you seen John?'

'No, I've not.'

Scarlet gestured to the broth. 'We thought you would have delivered that lot by now.'

'Bethla has had to keep some of the food separate. Some she's tainted, some she hasn't. It took a bit longer than she was expecting.'

'Right, well get it to the guards and while you're there, distract them so I can go to the dungeons.'

Will leant convincingly on his crutch as Much hurried on his way.

***

The guard room was busy. Some of the men on the night watch were just returning to rest while the others were about to begin their day's duties. There was loud talk and a jovial atmosphere, mainly about Sir Guy's luck on finding such a lusty wench to marry, even though she was *only* a Saxon commoner.

When Much entered with their breakfast, they were grateful and accepting of him. The idea of being surrounded by so many who'd wish him dead, made Much's hand's shake a little as he ladled the broth into bowls scattered across the table. He did not speak, even though they tried to engage with him. He simply smiled as though he was a mute simpleton. But the guards didn't care; they were just glad to be eating.

Meanwhile, Will hobbled past the archway and down to the gaol complex beneath the castle. The arrival of food also meant that, temporarily, the guard on the entrance to the cells was absent, and Will found his route clear. It wouldn't be for long though and he needed to be quick. John *had* to be here somewhere.

'Come on, come on, where are you, you big lout?' Will muttered under his breath. He peered down into the grate that was the only way in and out of the hole where most of the sheriff's prisoners ended up. 'John… John…!'

When no one answered his call, Will moved on to the other, smaller cells. They were empty. *Where is he?*

Will glanced back through his bandages to see if any guards were returning. None yet. He had a few more moments. The corridor curled down and around, getting narrower and darker. His pulse quickened. If he was spotted, there wasn't another way out apart from the way he had come in.

Pressing on, Will found that the corridor widened out, leading to a long wall of bars and a much larger single cell. A grated rectangular hole at the base of the far wall allowed meagre daylight. There, standing in half-shadow, was Little John. Will gasped. He was in a bad way; bruised, battered, his wide shoulders hunched. He looked like a broken man, whose spirit had been beaten from him.

'John…' Will said, removing his disguise.

John stepped out of the gloom in disbelief. 'Will?'

'We'd heard you were dead.' Will stretched an arm through the bars and John grabbed it like it was a lifeline.

'I'd heard that, too.' John tried to smile.

'We've been in worse scrapes.' Will put his crutch down and looked at the barred door. A bolt was locked across it.

'They keep the key on the wall behind you,' John said, his bruised and split lips making him wince. 'On a nail.'

'How convenient.' Will grabbed it, making easy use of the bolt. He tried to slide it back as quietly as he could.

'No one comes down this far.' The relief John felt when that door swung wide was immense but there was still a heavy weight upon his heart.

Will saw the desperate look in his friend's eye. 'Meg, she ain't married yet. There's still time!'

That was all that John needed to hear. He breathed out and straightened his back. 'Come on then!'

Together, they padded back up the corridor and past the other cells, past the guard room where they were finishing their meal and to the open door to the rest of the castle. Much had since returned to the kitchens and Will brought John up to date on the rest of the group's movements.

'And you trust this Bethla to do what she agreed?' John asked.

Will raised a hand. 'Listen.'

John did so but could hear nothing. He frowned.

Will beckoned him back inside. 'Let's have a look…'

'Are you mad? We need to get out of here.'

But Will continued towards the guard room. There was no movement or sound from the soldiers beyond snoring.

'By all that's…' John stifled a laugh.

The guards were unconscious, every one of them.

Bethla's potion had worked.

CHAPTER 14

The cock crowed.

Flanked by two soldiers, the Lord High Sheriff of Nottingham strode out into the upper ward, the stirring throng opening up before him. He was dressed in his finest livery.

The sun was just beginning to appear on the lip of the battlements and the morning dew had yet to leave the ground.

The sheriff mounted the gallows and a trumpeter blared a shrill series of notes, hushing the crowd into silence.

Stood only a few feet from de Rainault, Robin could see Marion hidden in the crowd on the opposite side of the gallows. Will, with John, now dressed as a beggar, stooping to disguise his height, was nearby.

'You are about to see a spectacle,' the sheriff began. 'Either Sir Guy of Gisburne will marry Meg of Wickham, under the watchful eyes of Our Lord Saviour, or that same female will swing from the rope for disobeying the will of the Church!'

'Get on with it!' A cry came from the crowds. The sheriff spun round to see where it had come from, but there was only a half-blind old beggar with a crutch leering through his bandages.

'Bring the woman!' The sheriff yelled an order to his men. Seconds later Meg was dragged out to the gallows, to the jeering of the crowd.

John's mouth dropped open. Meg's thick auburn hair was braided and she had flowers intertwined with her parted fringe. The red wedding dress she wore, embroidered with pearl leaves, cascaded down over her hips to the wooden slats of the gallows. The sun had risen over the castle walls, bathing her in its glory.

'She's…beautiful,' John straightened up as he breathed; forgetting himself for a moment and the plan to stay in disguise.

Will nudged John sharply as he hunched over again.

'I ask you now,' the sheriff called so that the crowds could hear, 'Meg of Wickham, do you intend to marry Sir Guy? Answer me! The length of your future will be determined by your response.'

Meg's eyes scanned the throng for any sign of the outlaws but she found none. John wanted to signal to her but he dare not.

'Come on, lass,' John said under his breath. 'Come on…'

'I will marry him,' Meg replied, her voice beginning to break. 'My John is dead. I have no choice.'

She thought him dead, too? John glanced down at Will. Was that why she'd agreed to marry Gisburne?

The crowd cheered. The wedding was going to happen! The sheriff took Meg's elbow and stepped back.

'Then I invite you all to join us in the great hall.' He leant towards the trembling bride and said so no one would hear, 'Change your mind now and you'll be dead before you step off these gallows.'

The throng clapped and waved. De Rainault tried to smile, but the expression never came naturally to him, so he glared at the peasants instead as he swept Meg into the castle. The people followed, Marion and the rest of the outlaws with them.

Soon the great hall was packed with people, including soldiers in disguise and as many peasants who could be squeezed in before the doors were closed. Food adorned the tables, fruits, roasted meats, and gallons of wine. It was a feast fit for a king let alone a bride and groom.

Standing in an alcove specially decorated with flowers and large candles, was Sir Guy, his armour gleaming. He knew he looked impressive and stood with a poise that the sheriff had not seen before. Next to him was the minister, bearded and tanned, long black hair messy around his face.

The sheriff manhandled Meg to her place in front of Gisburne. She couldn't bear to look at him.

'Dearly beloved,' began the minister, his prayer book open and in his palms. 'We are gathered here today to join this man and this woman together in Holy Matrimony…'

The sheriff's attentions were drawn away from the minister by the vile scum in his castle. They had already started consuming the wine and pulling off great chunks of meat. At this rate, it would all be gone before the outlaws made their appearance.

The minister eventually finished his lengthy reading and had wrapped a cord around the clasped hands of Guy and Meg.

Meg's hands were shaking and she felt disgust at the clamminess of Gisburne's palms.

The minister prompted Gisburne to begin speaking.

'I, Guy Alastair, take thee, Megan Claire, to be my wedded wife, to have and to hold from this day forward, for better for worse, for richer, for poorer, for fairer or fouler, in sickness and in health, to love and to cherish, till death us depart, according to God's holy ordinance; and thereunto I plight thee my troth.'

The minister motioned for Meg to take the vows. She faltered, the words catching in her throat.

'You need to say the vows, m'lady,' the minister prompted.

'Come on, woman. Out with it. This whole debacle is a farce!' said the sheriff as he turned to the captain, who stood at his shoulder. 'Flynn, they're not coming.'

'My Lord?'

'The outlaws! They have no interest in this woman. They are *not* coming to rescue her!'

'Meg,' Gisburne looked at his bride. 'Please, complete the vows.'

'Gisburne,' the sheriff growled. 'What are you playing at? This hasn't worked. Let's end this now. I'll kill that brother of mine!'

'If she doesn't want to complete her vows, I cannot force her,' the minister said quickly.

Gisburne drew his sword and brought it up to the minister's bushy beard. 'The ceremony *will* be completed.'

'Why, Gisburne, I didn't realise you were so desperate,' sneered the sheriff.

Meg looked at the minister, then to the sheriff and finally Gisburne. How *could* she go through with this? Was this really a better option than hanging? And perhaps worst of all, none of John's friends were coming for her. Her heart sank even further. The minister squinted at her from under his thick eyebrows.

Suddenly, there was a thud behind them. The wedding party turned to see that somebody in the congregation had toppled over, crashing to the floor.

Will, shuffling close, glanced at the fallen woman. Next to her, a man was daubing sweat from his brow. Three seconds later, he too tumbled to the floor.

Pulling his attention back from their audience, Gisburne brandished his sword, urging the minister to carry on.

'My Lord, the lady has to say the vows or this—'

'Meg,' interrupted Gisburne, 'there is a noose waiting for you. If you do not say the words, then I will end this minister's life as well as yours. Now speak!'

Meg swallowed hard. She couldn't have an innocent man's life on her conscience, even though she'd be marrying a monster. The notion chilled her.

Through gentle sobs she began to speak. 'I, Megan Claire, take thee… Guy… Alastair, to be… to be my—'

Another person collapsed not far from where Meg was standing.

'What is going on?' hissed the sheriff. 'You're both taking so long the crowd is beginning to expire from the heat in here. There was more drama in that dreary play of the king's I had to sit through. I didn't imagine a wedding to be worse.'

From the crowd, Will looked over to Marion and smiled. Bethla's potion was taking effect. Soon the sheriff and Gisburne would be out cold, as would most of the congregation which, the outlaws hoped, included the undercover soldiers. They would simply be able to walk out of the castle!

'…to be my wedded husband, to have and to hold from this day forward, for better for worse, for richer, for poorer, for fairer or fouler, in sickness and in health, to love and to cherish, till death us depart, according to God's holy ordinance; and thereunto I plight thee my troth.'

'Then,' said the minister, 'it is my duty to… my duty to…'

'Minister, are you quite well?' The sheriff looked at the man and then down at the sweat that was forming on the backs of his own hands.

'Complete the ceremony!' bellowed Gisburne.

'Captain…' Turning to Flynn, the sheriff barked, 'this is a shambles! The outlaws aren't…'

He didn't finish the sentence. His body folded at the knees, and he fell to floor; he was out cold.

'My Lord Sheriff!' As Flynn knelt to his master, he saw the crippled beggar throw his crutch to one side. Immediately he straightened up again, his eyes fixed on the crowd.

Seeing Flynn was close to recognising them, Will acted, 'Come on John. This is it!'

As John shrugged off his disguise and surged forward, Flynn shouts across the hall, 'Wolfshead!'

Meg burst into tears of joy and relief as her beloved John crashed through the dazed crowd to her side. *He's alive! And the minister hasn't yet fin-*

'I now pronounce you man and wife.' The minister muttered as he too passed out.

John stared in horror at the unconscious man of the cloth. It was too late.

Gisburne was laughing. Meg was beyond distraught.

Sir Guy and Lady Meg.

Husband and wife.

'I'll kill you, Gisburne!' John went to grab the knife at his hip but missed it. He tried again but his hand wouldn't connect. He suddenly felt as if he'd drunk too much ale. 'Meg...' John shook his head, trying to get rid of the feeling, but his feet were becoming heavier. 'What's—?'

Meg screamed as John collapsed in a heap before her.

Will, who'd been about to rush to John's side, turned instead to Marion, just in time to see her fall too. Clutching at his own head, his vision beginning to blur, Scarlet turned to stare at Bethla. She was standing at the end of the length of tables. Her arms folded. Much was fast asleep at her feet.

She was smiling.

'What have you done, you double-crossing...?' Will was unconscious before he hit the ground.

Bethla walked calmly up to the new bride and groom. Stepping over the fallen bodies, she held out her hand. Into her waiting palm Gisburne dropped a heavy purse of coins into her hand. 'You did well. Now leave and don't come back. The villagers of Shirebook won't trouble you again.'

Bethla nodded and spun on her heels. Stepping over the minister, she looked pityingly at Will. She'd quite liked the brief time they'd spent together. Better him than that simpleton Much they'd lumbered her with.

Weighing the purse in her hands, enjoying the way its contents settled between her palms, Bethla walked away.

***

Flynn looked down at the fallen sheriff, and then at the sea of collapsed guests. It had all happened so fast. He turned to speak to Sir Guy, but Meg got there first.

'You lied to me!' she screamed at Gisburne. 'You told me John was dead!'

'My Lord, I don't understand,' Flynn pushed in front of Meg, as he stared around the great hall.

'You don't need to understand, Captain, you just need to do what I tell you. Now, prepare fresh horses,' ordered Gisburne, 'my wife and I are leaving.'

CHAPTER 15

Tuck and Nasir had waited outside the castle, concealed by a line of trees. When Robin and the other didn't show, and the sounds of revelry that has been coming from the castle had gone suspiciously quiet, Nasir had decided to investigate. It didn't take him long to work out what had happened.

Running back to fetch Tuck, the two outlaws had worked quickly, pulling the unconscious bodies of their friends from the tangle of fallen arms and legs strewn across the courtyard, corridors and the great hall itself.

Now, travelling fast on a cart purloined from the grounds, Nasir steered them deep into Sherwood, the canopy of trees enveloping them in its secure embrace.

On the flat bed of the cart, the sleeping outlaws began to come round. Will was the first to regain consciousness, his disorientation quickly replaced with grunts and curses as Marion, Much, John, Edward and finally Robin woke from their sleep.

'Seeing you all lying there,' Nasir said, 'I feared the worst.'

'I can't believe Bethla double-crossed us!' Will rubbed his pounding head. 'Didn't you realise she was up to something, Much?'

'Bethla said she wanted to make sure the right food was put in the right places herself, so that not everyone ate what she'd tainted,' Much replied. He felt responsible for what had happened but Bethla had seemed so grateful that he and Will had taken her away from that awful imprisonment, he hadn't suspected a thing. 'She was just so... nice.'

'It's not your fault, Much,' said Robin.

'Thanks Robin,' Much mumbled, before adding, 'you look strange with black hair!'

Robin smiled. Black streaks where the charcoal was running had begun to appear at his temples and down his neck.

'So Gisburne and Meg...' Much risked a glance at John. He was sat at the back of the cart, his legs hanging over the edge. He said nothing as Much ventured, 'They're really married, then?'

Robin watched John's back. The big man's shoulders where hunched, and his head hung down in despair.

'Nasir...' Robin moved up front to sit next to the Saracen, exchanging places with Tuck who settled next to Marion. 'There was no sign of Meg or Gisburne in the great hall?'

'No sign.'

'I reckon that witch Bethla's got them!' exclaimed Will.

'What would she want with them?' asked Tuck.

'Perhaps they're in another part of the castle?' Much reasoned.

'Nah,' Will disagreed. 'They've gone. Gisburne's taken her off somewhere.'

'We will get her back,' Robin said, speaking louder so John could hear.

Little John didn't turn around. He didn't want the others to see the tears streaming down his face. His Meg, his bride-to-be, taken from under his protection by that snake Gisburne. He'd failed her. Even if they did manage to find her and take her back to Wickham, why would she want to marry him now? Perhaps Meg had been right... marrying an outlaw wasn't for the best.

While John struggled to stifle his sobs, Marion motioned for Robin to let him be for now.

The outlaws sat in silence for the rest of the journey to the camp, wondering what to do and where to start the search for Meg.

***

'Good God!'

Hugo entered the great hall, appalled by what he saw. It was like the aftermath of a drunken banquet, except it wasn't even noon and the feast had only started five hours ago.

His brother, the sheriff, was propped up against a table leg cradling his head in his hands. Hugo looked around with disgust at the commoners that surrounded him as he slapped Robert's face.

'Oh, leave me alone!' the sheriff complained.

'Where is Gisburne? Where are the outlaws?'

Looking up at his brother, de Rainault grimaced. 'It was a trick! The wolfsheads poisoned everyone.'

'How?'

'The food! The drink!' The sheriff struggled to his feet, angry and incensed. 'They must have taken Gisburne and his wife with them.'

'His wife?'

'Yes, Hugo. You did hear me correctly. Gisburne's wife!'

Hugo mouth dropped. 'He went through with the whole thing?'

'He couldn't get the words out quick enough! It was as if...' The sheriff's voice tailed off. A thought had interrupted him. 'No...surely not!'

'What, brother?'

'It was as if Gisburne knew we were all going to pass out!'

'But that sounds like he was in league with the outlaws!'

Robert de Rainault straightened his tunic, the ache in his head clearing with every turning of his mind. 'He's changed since he came back from Normandy. Something's got into him. But I can't imagine even Gisburne, as weak-kneed as he is, would join the outlaws! And why would they have allowed the wedding to have happened? Unless they have no allegiance to the Wickham woman after all.'

'The Pagan heretics! They have no concept of marriage.'

'That may be so, but that still leave us with a problem.'

'Us, Robert?'

'Yes. Us. This was all your idea, brother. I haven't so much as gained a new member of the household as lost a steward.'

'You'd got used to him not being around. If he's gone again, let him be.'

'Yes, but Jonas is dead from the hunting trip and Flynn isn't fully trained as captain yet. As much as it pains me to say...' The sheriff's eyes widened in an expression that the abbot knew signified an obsessive plan was hatching in his brother's head.

'What do you intend to do?' Hugo asked.

'Gisburne will not make a fool out of me! He needs to be brought back.'

'And how do you intend to do that? You don't even know where he's gone.'

'Like I said, it's impossible he has joined the outlaws. But it *is* possible they helped him for the woman's sake. So if anyone knows where he's gone, it's Robin Hood!'

***

'Gisburne could be anywhere.' Robin stared into the fire that crackled and popped, the heat prickling the skin on his face.

'Don't let John see you disheartened like this when he gets back from the lake.' Marion stifled a sigh as she stroked the hair that fell across Robin's shoulders, blonde again now that the charcoal had been washed out.

Robin shook his head. 'Of course I won't. Tuck...'

'Yes, Robin?' Tuck put down the lengths of spruce he was scraping into arrows.

'That minister you detained for a while, did he indicate he knew Gisburne?'

'No. Father Apollinari was summoned by the Abbot Hugo to perform the marriage. Why?'

'Just looking for clues to Meg's whereabouts. If this minister knew Gisburne, if that was why he was asked to be there, he may have known where he went.'

Nasir moved towards them, looking over at John who hadn't entered the circle around the fire since they'd returned from the castle. 'The minister...he knew of no one at the castle. He only knew the abbot.'

'Then we need to get our eyes and ears out,' Marion said.

'Yes, get word to the villages,' Robin agreed. 'See if anyone has seen them.'

'He could have taken Meg anywhere,' Tuck added forlornly.

'Even back to Normandy.' Nasir stoked the fire with his foot. 'But we must not give up hope.'

'Will, Much...' called Robin.

Gathered together, Robin gave instructions to each of them. They were to visit the neighbouring villages, towns and shires, to ask if Sir Guy and his new wife had been seen.

***

Once his friends had dispersed, Robin went to find John at his favourite spot by the lake. 'No matter how long it takes, we *will* get Meg back. I promise you that.'

John looked at Robin with a sad shake of his head. 'You can't promise me that.'

'But I do,' Robin insisted. 'You never gave up on me when Marion left us. You never gave up hope that everything would be alright. And here we are, together again. Doesn't that count for something?'

John threw a stone into the water, watching the ripples disperse. 'Aye, lad. But Meg isn't one of us. She isn't for the outlaw life.'

'But she *is* one of us,' Robin said. 'In her heart, like Edward, she has the spirit to fight against our oppressors. To the sheriff, to the king, we're *all* outlaws. Now would she want you to sit there and feel sorry for yourself?'

'Don't tell me what she wants!'

'Why shouldn't I?'

'Because you don't know Meg like I do!'

'No, I don't.' Robin patted his friend's shoulder. 'But I do know that she loves you, John, and wherever she is right now, she's hurting. She needs you. We need you.'

John stood, brushing dry leaves from the backs of his legs. He stared into the trees. 'Do you know what Herne said to me? "Captured all or captured none." He wasn't just talking about us.'

Robin smiled. He knew full-well that Herne's words often had meanings that weren't clear. 'And what was he talking about?'

'That Meg has captured all of *me*.'

'Then let's go and get her back,' Robin said, holding out a hand to his friend.

John looked at the offering and smiled. He gripped Robin's hand tight. *Together we.*

CHAPTER 16

Days turned into weeks and, while the sheriff seethed and ranted in Nottingham castle, waiting for news from his own soldiers searching for Gisburne, no word reached Robin's ears either. The whole of Sherwood, and far beyond, knew the outlaw wanted to find Gisburne, and that they stood him accused of abducting Meg of Wickham – but no news came to the forest.

There was nothing until one day, when the summer nights had shortened and the first of the autumn leaves fell, Edward summoned the outlaws to Wickham.

'He's gone home.' Edward announced.

'Home?' John frowned.

'To Gisburne village.'

'But that was one of the first places we looked,' Much said.

'He has been moving around,' Nasir reasoned, 'thinking we will give up.'

'Aye, well he's wrong!' replied John.

'He don't know us well, does he?' Will folded his arms, angry at the weeks they'd spent searching in vain.

'Or he knows us too well,' said Robin. 'If word reaches him that he's been seen in Gisburne village, he may move on again. Edward, how did this information reach you?'

'I know people in Heysham. They were taking goods from the seaport across to Gisburne. They saw him talking to some of the landowners.'

'Getting himself a new master?' Will sneered. 'Well let's go get him.'

'Did your contact say they saw Meg?' John asked.

'No, John, I'm sorry, they didn't,' Edward said sadly.

'That doesn't mean anything,' offered Robin. 'Meg could be—'

'A prisoner?' John growled. 'That makes it worse!'

'Then we can't delay,' Marion said. 'We've been waiting for word for so long. Let's head out in the morning.'

'No.' replied Robin. 'We go now, through the night.'

'I can give you fresh horses,' offered Edward.

'Thank you,' said Marion.

'No more than a day's ride,' Nasir said.

'Trade them if you need to,' Edward added. 'Just bring Meg home.'

John clasped Edward's arm. 'Aye, we will.'

'Then good luck to you all, my friends. May Herne protect you.'

***

The next day, at first light, they came up over the ridge that connected Preston through to the abbey at Bolton. Bowland Forest stretched before them, appearing more impressive and denser than Sherwood.

Below them sat the village of Gisburne. It was a hamlet of only a few hundred people and therefore, Robin hoped, it would be fairly easy to find Sir Guy. He also hoped that news of their arrival hadn't preceded them.

As they looked down upon the village, all seemed calm and quiet as Will asked, 'Do we announce our presence or what?'

'We'll keep watch over the place from here until sunset,' said Robin. 'There's only one road in and out, so we'll see anyone coming or going.'

John was as eager as Will to storm down the hill, swords flashing and with revenge in their hearts, but Robin was insistent.

'We need to have the advantage. We go down there now and Meg could be put in danger.'

Much was just about to collect some firewood when Tuck stopped him. 'They'll see the fire. It'll give away that someone's up here.'

'Tuck's right,' said Marion. 'I know it's getting cold, but it's only a couple more hours until dusk.'

Much returned to the ground next to her. 'Do you think John will be alright?'

Marion lowered her voice in concern. 'I hope more than anything that Meg is safe. If she's not, then I don't think even Will could hold John back.'

***

Sir Guy had assured Bernard, the Earl of Barnoldswick, who governed the surrounding villages, that he and his wife would be temporary residents and so had been allowed to take lodgings in the outhouse towards the back of Bernard's estate.

81

The earl, however, hadn't welcomed Sir Guy with open arms. He'd known Gisburne many years ago and their relationship had soured soon after Sir Guy had become the Sheriff of Nottingham's steward. Robert de Rainault had once tried to spread his influence far beyond his remit of Nottinghamshire and had used his new steward's familial roots to gain access to chattels and wealth. But Bernard had kept the greedy sheriff at bay, using his own influence with King Richard to put de Rainault back in his place. De Rainault had withdrawn but not after attempting to double-cross the earl by spreading vicious rumours about him within both the Royal Court and the Church.

Bernard, therefore, have been somewhat shocked when, a few weeks ago, he'd seen two horses make their way slowly down from the ridge with Sir Guy on one and a woman, who looked like she'd been dressed for a wedding, on the other. Bernard was even more surprised when Sir Guy announced the woman as his wife. The obvious fact that she'd been crying for quite a long time was quietly ignored by both parties.

As time progressed and Sir Guy gave no indication of his impending movements, Bernard decided to find out what was going on for himself.

Gathering a few of his men to accompany him, the earl travelled into the village that evening. He banged on the door of the large outhouse with a gloved fist.

'Sir Guy, I would speak with you.' His voice was carried off on the strong breeze so he tried again. 'Sir Guy!'

Eventually the door opened and the heat from the open fireplace rushed out. Guy looked out at him, frowning, suspicious and wary. He looked dishevelled and tired.

'Are you well, man?' Bernard asked.

'What do you want?' Gisburne replied.

'It's been nigh on two months since you arrived. I would request you tell me when you plan to leave.'

'When we are ready.'

'And Lady Gisburne?'

'She is well,' Gisburne replied quickly…*too* quickly, Bernard felt.

'May I see her?'

'You may not.'

'May I ask why?'

'Is a husband to explain why his wife does not wish to be disturbed?'

'Does not or cannot?'

Gisburne looked pensive. 'What are you suggesting?'

'I'm suggesting nothing, Sir Guy. I merely enquire as to the health of Lady Gisburne. We have seen you in the village from time to time, although you have ignored most of the villagers. Yet no one has seen Lady Gisburne since you arrived.' Bernard paused, waiting for Sir Guy to respond. 'So I ask you, Sir Guy: is Lady Gisburne well?'

'She is well,' Gisburne said again. 'Now leave us be.'

As the door was about to close, Bernard wedged a booted foot in. Gisburne looked down at it, scowling.

'I am afraid I cannot do that,' Bernard said, his grey hair blowing in the wind. His dark eyes narrowed. 'You are on my land in my property. If you will not allow me access I shall order my men here to in break past you.'

Gisburne considered what he was saying then nodded once. 'A moment. If it's just you, my Lord.'

Bernard agreed and removed his foot. The door shut then opened again a few moments later.

Leaving his guard outside, Bernard entered the building as Gisburne stepped back, closing the door behind him. It was one room, with a large bed, a table and two chairs. The fire in the grate was burning fiercely. At the table was Lady Gisburne, apparently still in her wedding dress which was now filthy and ripped in places. A bundle of other dresses, clean, unworn and untouched, were on the floor by the bed.

Bernard noticed the length of rope by the fireplace, one end tied around a leg of the bed, the other loose.

'Lady Gisburne,' Bernard said, nodding to her.

Meg did not look up.

'She has not slept well,' Gisburne said.

'And it appears neither have you. Look at the state of you, man!' Bernard shook his head. 'Look at the state of both of you!'

'We are both well. I assure you that we will be leaving soon.'

'And go where?' Bernard looked at Meg then back at Gisburne. 'I've known you for many years, Guy. I know that we have not spoken for the last few of those for reasons you are fully aware of, but you came here clearly seeking refuge, yet you refuse and resist any help. You have shut yourselves away.'

'Lady Gisburne...'

'She does not take kindly to strangers.'

Bernard sighed. He didn't believe that but knew that he would get nowhere for the moment. He was satisfied for now that Lady Gisburne was seemingly unharmed, if a little reclusive. Perhaps she *didn't* like strangers?

Bernard nodded his retreat and Gisburne nodded back.

'If there I anything I can do for you, Lady Gisburne,' he said, 'I am at your disposal at the main house.'

The door closed behind him and the earl found himself buffeted by the wind as he made his way back up the path to his home.

***

Gisburne watched through the crack in the door as the earl moving off.

'How long is this going to go on for?' Meg asked, face caked with dirt. Her tears had long ago dried. In fact, she hadn't cried for weeks. 'He'll come back and with soldiers.'

'We will be gone long before then.'

'We can't keep travelling.' Meg winced as Gisburne grabbed her, walked her over to the bed and tied the rope back around her sore wrists, the other end still tight to the bed leg. He didn't look at her. He never looked at her. 'Why did you go through with the wedding?'

It was a question she'd asked him over and over again since they'd first left Nottingham. He either ignored it or never answered at all. And once more, there was no response. 'Are you hungry?' was all he asked.

'It wasn't through desire or love,' Meg continued. 'I am at least grateful you haven't…you know…'

'I would not do that,' Gisburne replied.

'Then why?' Meg sighed. 'This hasn't turned out as you'd hoped, has it?'

'I don't know what you mean.'

At last, he was responding. Perhaps she was getting through to him. Perhaps he was tired of all this too.

'Our marriage was just to get John and Robin and the others. But *you* changed the plan. *You* arranged for everyone to be poisoned.'

'You think I did that?'

Meg nodded. 'I'm convinced of it. I've had enough time tied to this bed to do nothing but think!'

Gisburne moved to the fire, stoked it a few times and then sat on the floor, staring deep into the flames.

CHAPTER 17

'Who are you?'

Bethla hadn't expected anyone from upstairs to return to the kitchens once they'd satisfied themselves all was in hand, let alone Gisburne himself.

'I'm no one,' she replied, getting on with kneading dough. She knew Much was about to return any moment now with a sack of apples so hoped this conversation would not take long.

'No one, eh?' Gisburne replied, looking her up and down. It wasn't with interest, it was with suspicion. 'I've not seen you around here before. How long have you been here?'

'Only a little while,' Bethla replied vaguely.

'And you happen to have experience in running a castle's kitchen?'

'Some.' She moved along the table to grab some for flour, dusting the surface down. It didn't seem to bother her that Gisburne was in her way. She just pushed past him.

'And you also happen to be available to take the cook's place when he suddenly falls ill?'

She looked up at him, wiping her cheek with a sleeve. A line of flour appeared under her right eye. 'If I didn't you'd be having nothing but raw meat for your wedding banquet. Who else could prepare it? You?'

'Well…no…but that's not what I'm saying.'

'Then, my Lord, what are you saying? I'm very busy and there is still much to do.'

Gisburne grabbed her arm and forced her around to face him.

'Ow! You're hurting me!'

'You're here with them, aren't you?' He leant in close and Bethla could smell the wine on his breath. 'They've put you to work in the kitchens. For what reason?'

'Get off me! I don't know what you're talking about!'

'Tell me or I'll have you removed and taken to the dungeon. You'll talk down there soon enough.'

'And who would cook your meats?'

Gisburne squeezed her arm tighter. He wasn't in the mood for games.

'Where do you want these put, Bethla?'

Gisburne tensed, as did Bethla. He recognised that voice but he didn't turn around. So she was here with the outlaws. He didn't need to see Much to know that was him. So he pretended he was oblivious to his identity. 'Answer the boy...'

'Over there, by the carrots,' Bethla replied to Much.

But Much knew that figure leaning over Bethla. Gisburne obviously hadn't recognised him because he hadn't turned around or called for the guards. Much quickly put the sack down and made himself scarce.

Gisburne waited for Much to leave before releasing Bethla.

'How much are they paying you?'

'They're not paying me anything,' Bethla replied, rubbing her arm.

'Don't lie to me! You're here to...to poison the food! Is that it?'

Bethla's silence told Gisburne all he needed to know.

'I should take you before the sheriff,' he replied. Then he thought for a moment. 'Why did they choose you? What did they offer you? If they're paying you, I can double it...triple it. But you need to do something for me.'

***

'I've long thought about coming back here, to this village where I grew up. But I knew the sheriff wouldn't release me from his service. When the Abbot Hugo cooked up the ridiculous plan that you and I pretend to get married, it dawned on me that you were my way out.'

'So you married me knowing the sheriff wouldn't want a wife following you around?'

Meg thought she saw a glint of a smile on Gisburne's face. 'Something like that.'

'So why are we hiding out here? Why aren't we dining with the earl and his wife? Why aren't you doing everything you can to put yourself in good stead with him? He seems like a gentle man.'

'Bernard is an honest man.'

'Then be like him. Be honest. Don't be like the sheriff.'

'I am not like the sheriff!' Gisburne spat, the calmness in his voice gone.

'Do you think John and the others see the difference?'

'I don't care what they see! They are outlaws. Their opinions don't concern me.'

'They may be outlaws in your eyes, but they would never keep someone a prisoner as you have kept me.'

Gisburne leant on his right arm, the unswept floor pressing grit into his palm. Keeping Meg like this was never his intention. In fact, he never considered how this was going to go once he'd decided to push the minister into completing the vows.

'It will have to do.'

Meg rubbed her wrists, skin red where the rope chafed. 'If you think that keeping me with you will eventually make me *want* to be with you then you're wrong. I love John and these ropes and those vows we said won't ever change that.'

'He's not coming for you. No one is,' Gisburne snarled. 'You are my wife now.'

***

Sir Bernard was about to blow out his candle and settle down for the night when there came a thumping at his door. Cursing, he listened out for one of the servants to open it, heard a muffled exchange of voices and decided it was important. Pulling a shawl over his shoulders, he left his wife, Lady Irene, to sleep and headed out of their room to see who it was.

Two soldiers, apologetic for disturbing him, stood there, hands on their hilts.

'My Lord,' one of them, 'you asked to be notified in relation to anything concerning Sir Guy.'

'Yes, that's correct. What has happened?' Bernard feared for Lady Gisburne's safety.

'Some of the villagers have been approached by strangers asking about Sir Guy.'

'What did they want to know?'

'I have one of them waiting outside if you'd care to talk to them?'

'One of the strangers or one of the villagers?'

'One of the villagers, my Lord.'

Bernard ordered them sent in. It was young Kevin, the son of the village's granary steward. He was nervous about being before his earl, but Bernard kindly bade him sit and offered him some wine.

'Now, Kevin, tell me what happened?'

'Well, my Lord,' the boy began, 'Daniel came in and said he'd seen some men up on the ridge.'

'Daniel?'

'My brother.'

'Yes, of course. Please, continue…'

'So we sneaked out to have a look and three of them were headed this way.'

'Did they harm you?'

'No. They were nice,' Kevin said. 'They asked about a blonde man who had come here with a woman.'

'What did you say?'

'We said we didn't know anything about anybody.'

'Good boy,' said Bernard and tossed the lad a coin. 'Now run along home and no more night trips to the ridge. They could have been outlaws!'

As Kevin gleefully cradled the coin and dashed out towards his home, Bernard turned to the guards. 'Go to the ridge and if these strangers are there, invite them back here.'

'Now sir?'

'Yes, now.'

'To here?'

'Is there a problem?'

The guards shook their heads, but it was the middle of the night and bringing strangers to the earl's home was unusual. Orders, though, were orders.

Bernard didn't have to wait long for the guards' return and he was surprised to see a woman had come with them, dressed in the colours of the woodlands, red hair tied in a ponytail and a long-bow over her shoulder, a full quiver hanging down her back. Behind her were two men, one, with long blonde hair and dressed in dark browns with a unique form of circular chainmail covering his leather tunic, also armed with a longbow and arrows but with a sword at his hip, and a tall man, unkempt, in sleeveless fur outerwear. He held a quarterstaff. He looked angry, while the woman appeared wary and the shorter blonde man self-assured. He seemed to be their leader and, as Bernard took this all in, he decided they weren't nobility, or perhaps in the case of two of them, had shied away from their class.

'I am Robin of Sherwood, this is Marion and John.'

'I am unaccustomed to having armed strangers in my home at the dead of night but something tells me that you are not here to cause us trouble.' Bernard looked between them all. 'In fact, I think you might be here to help me with a problem I've been lumbered with.'

'Perhaps,' Robin said.

'Is Gisburne here?' John asked gruffly.

'Can I offer you refreshment? Sherwood is a way from here and you must be tired.'

Robin stepped forward. 'Thank you for your hospitality, my Lord, but we need to have this information now.'

'A woman's life may depend on it,' Marion said.

Bernard nodded thoughtfully. 'The Lady Gisburne.'

John clenched his quarterstaff and his teeth. Robin shot out an arm to hold him back. 'We know that…Lady Gisburne…has been taken against her will. We mean to rescue her from her predicament. We come willingly here to talk to you. We mean you no harm and no disservice. If you are unsure of our honour, we have horses we can offer you as a show of goodwill. I'm sure that you can appreciate that, giving up our rides home will make our journey longer and more treacherous.'

'What do you intend to do with Sir Guy?'

'So he *is* here!' John growled.

'Yes,' nodded Bernard. 'Sir Guy may hold our village in his title, but we are not like him, nor his superior, Robert de Rainault. I take it you know of him, too?'

'We've clashed once or twice,' responded Robin dryly.

'Then you understand we hold no allegiance to Sir Guy?' 'Do you want us to remove Sir Guy, my Lord?' Marion asked.

'We'll do more than remove him!' added John.

Robin raised a finger to silence the big man. 'The woman, her name is Meg, is our priority. She is our friend and was taken from us under false pretences. If Sir Guy confronts us, we wish no bloodshed beyond our concerns with him personally.'

'Then you have my blessing to go onto my land to retrieve your friend,' Bernard agreed, and motioned for the three newcomers to leave, 'but know this…'

Robin, Marion and John turned. 'My Lord?' Robin said.

'If your skirmish spills out onto the streets, my guards will cut you down. All of you.'

CHAPTER 18

There was only one door to the outhouse and Robin and Marion stood some distance away from it, longbows drawn back and arrows nocked. Will and Nasir hid either side of the door, swords ready, while John brought up the rear with Tuck and Much holding burning torches. Bernard's guards watched and waited.

'Give it up, Guy! You're surrounded!' called Robin into the dark.

There was no response, so Robin tried again. 'We know you're in there. Send Meg out and no harm will come to you.'

'That's what he thinks…' hissed John.

All was quiet from the building so Robin let fly an arrow that embedded itself in the door, knowing Sir Guy would have heard it. A few moments later the door cracked open.

The wood panel moved slowly until, at last, the outlaws saw Meg. She was stood before Guy, a knife at her throat.

Gisburne looked at them wildly, not sure where they all were in the darkness of the night, the black pierced only by Much and Tuck's torches.

'Let her go, Guy!' Robin ordered.

An arrow, from Marion, landed at Gisburne's feet.

John stepped forward, seeing the fear on his beloved's face. 'It'll be alright, lass!' he called to her.

'John… John..!' Meg scanned the night, seeing John's shape outlined by the dancing flames.

'Quiet!' snarled Gisburne and held Meg tighter.

'How do you want this to end, Gisburne?' shouted Will. 'We can make it easy for you!'

The proximity of Will's voice took Gisburne by surprise and he stumbled back, dragging Meg with him.

Nasir nodded to Will and they both scrambled towards the door.

Letting go of Meg, Gisburne dived to the fireplace, grabbing his sword on the way.

Gisburne thrust at Will with both knife and sword, but Scarlet deftly ducked out of the way, leaving an opening for Nasir to tumble forwards and cross his twin swords, blocking Gisburne's strikes.

'Take her!' Nasir cried to Will, who darted forward, clutching hold of Meg and bundling her to the door.

John came thundering into the room, lifting Meg as though she were a doll and carrying her outside, leaving Will free to help Nasir. In seconds however, John was back, his quarterstaff raised.

'He's mine!' he roared and launched himself forward, knocking Nasir and Will aside as if they were skittles. He brought the quarterstaff down hard, aiming for Gisburne's skull.

Gisburne however, had been expecting the move, and rolled quickly out of the way. He dropped his knife as he brought his sword up to parry John's blows.

Little John's immense strength and the weight behind his arms rained down upon the knight who was weakening. Such was the outlaw's rage that Gisburne's sword was soon knocked from his hands, the blade clattering to the floor.

Guy cowered as John raised his quarterstaff for the final, fatal blow.

Just as the giant man began to swing the staff to deliver the final blow, Robin called out, 'No, John!'

'Get out of the way, lad!' John cried.

'No! Meg is safe!'

'But she's his! I'll free her from him! I'll make her a widow!'

Robin shouted at the top of his voice. 'They're not married, John!'

But John wasn't listening. He pulled his staff up over his head, increasing the momentum for when it would come down. Gisburne had heard, though, and was open mouthed, his arm lowering.

'What...what did you say?'

'You're not married to Meg,' Robin said. 'John...hear me...'

John frowned. 'But the minister...'

'That was me,' said Robin.

'You?' Gisburne and John said simultaneously.

'In disguise.'

'Why did you not say this sooner? You let me think she was married to Gisburne all this time?'

Tuck and Much appeared at the door. Marion followed with Meg.

'Nasir and I, we stopped the real minister on his way to Nottingham,' explained Tuck. 'Robin took his place while everyone was in the hall.'

'But you were dressed as a rat-catcher,' said Will.

'A rat-catcher to catch a rat,' Nasir nodded.

'I changed before we all went into the great hall,' explained Robin.

'Pity you didn't catch that rat Bethla before she knocked us all out,' added Will with a grin. 'So Meg gets to marry this big oaf, after all?'

John lowered his staff, confused as to why they hadn't told him Meg wasn't married to Gisburne, but soon a smile grew across his bearded face, a smile that became a grin, that became a snigger, that became a belly laugh. What did it matter now? He rushed to Meg who was stunned into relief and silence. Sweeping her up, he spun her around and they kissed, weeks of tension, fear, dread and despair wiped away.

'Are you hurt? Did he hurt you?' John asked through their passionate embrace.

'No, John. Apart from keeping me tied up, he never laid a finger on me.'

On the floor, Gisburne looked as relieved as John did. He wasn't shackled to the wench! But he soon tensed when he saw Will's sneer in his direction. 'What are you going to do to me?'

'Nothing,' said Robin.

'Nothing?' echoed Will incredulously. 'What do you mean: nothing?'

'Nothing,' Robin repeated. 'Just don't go back to Nottingham. And don't ever set foot in Sherwood again.'

Gisburne sat up, 'A wolfshead banishing *me*? Never.'

'If you don't agree to stay away,' Will snapped, 'I'll kill you myself right now.'

'You won't get away with this,' Gisburne said through painful winces.

'What? Allowing you to live?' asked Robin. 'You did what you did. You ran from Nottingham. So stay here. You are, after all, Sir Guy of *Gisburne*. So what better place to start a new life?'

Gisburne turned away, shame, regret and anger flowing through him as he watched the outlaws leave.

Sagging back against the floor, the heat from the fireplace warmed his back. He didn't know how long he had stayed there for, but it was still dark when he awoke suddenly.

Standing over him was a dark shape, a soldier, his chainmail glinting in the flames.

'Who...'

'Look at the state of you,' Flynn said.

'What… what are you doing here?'

Flynn pulled Gisburne to a sitting position and gave him water from his flask. 'I was sent here to get you.'

'Sent by whom?' Gisburne gasped. The water felt so good.

'Your superior.'

'The sheriff…' said Gisburne. 'He can go to Hell. How did you find me?'

'We followed Robin Hood.'

'We?'

'My men and I. We knew they'd received word of your whereabouts so we tracked them.' Flynn stood, hooking his flask back on his hip. 'You're coming back now.'

'I'm never going back to Nottingham.' Will's threat was still ringing in Gisburne's ears, but he wasn't afraid of a bullish outlaw. He knew that Robin had spoken sense. A new life. Something different. A change.

'Now that could be a problem,' Flynn said.

'Why? Can't the sheriff find another steward?'

'I'm the Captain of the Guard now Jonas has gone.'

'I know. So what?'

'And if I don't follow my orders the sheriff will make me his steward,' Flynn said. 'I could never be as good at is as you, Sir Guy.'

Dripping with sarcasm, Flynn's words hung in the air.

'I do not care.'

'There is one other thing.'

'Just go away!' exclaimed Gisburne.

'If you refuse, I have orders to kill you. And I know you don't want to die.'

Gisburne gritted his teeth. Flynn was right. 'And parade my body through the streets of Nottingham, no doubt.'

'So if you don't want to die and you refuse to come back with me, there's always this…'

Flynn reached inside his tunic and pulled out, to Gisburne's horror, a scrap of material, on it, on one side, embossed in gold, a sun motif.

'Where… did you get that?'

'So it is yours. Jonas was right.' Flynn held it up, the sun glowing in the firelight. 'I intend to do some investigations of my own about the significance of this piece of cloth and if you don't come willingly and quietly, I'll chain you up like a common outlaw and present you and this,' he continued, waving the material in Gisburne's face, 'to the sheriff. I'm sure he'll be as keen as I am to learn why you might want to keep such an innocent looking thing secret.'

EPILOGUE

Marion tugged the cord of Meg's wedding dress tight across her friend's back. It was raining outside and the cold was getting into everyone's bones, but the mood in Wickham that day was cheerful.

'I still can't believe you all came to rescue me.' Meg sat down to allow Marion to arrange her hair.

'Of course we did. Now it's time to start the next chapter in your life. Soon you'll be Meg Little,' Marion smiled, 'We've all looked forward to this for so long. John is so happy. And that's all down to you.'

The rain had eased by the time Meg was ready and she soon found herself on Edward's arm, with Marion following, walking to the barn where the good folk of Wickham had congregated.

John was waiting, upright and chest out, his stomach a knot of nerves. He could take on a whole contingent of soldiers without batting an eyelid, but right now...

Will nudged him as Meg came through the doors. 'Here she comes.'

'Aye, here she comes,' John's voice wobbled.

'She looks beautiful,' Robin whispered from where he stood next to Much and Nasir.

'Glad I suggested you comb your beard, now?' Will laughed.

'You look like a proper moppet now that you've actually shaved for once,' teased John in return.

As Meg reached the centre of the barn, the congregation formed a circle around them and Tuck stepped in, smiling from ear to ear.

'Don't look so nervous, John,' Meg said quietly, standing on his left. 'A big brave man like you.'

John's words got caught in his throat. He looked at her dress, tinted blue and weaved with winter flowers. It was far prettier than the one Gisburne had given her.

'I ask all here,' Tuck began, 'if there is any reason that they oppose this marriage?'

John glared at everyone within his sight, as if daring them to speak up.

'No?' Tuck nodded, 'I question you, then, John Clive and Megan Claire if there is any reason, any transgression that prohibits your union?'

'None, Tuck,' John said quietly.

'None!' said Meg brightly.

'Then I am pleased to say that we are gathered here today to join this man and this woman together in Holy Matrimony,' intoned Tuck. He wrapped a thin piece of blessed cloth around Meg and John's clasped hands. 'John Clive, please say your vows.'

'I, John Clive, take thee, Megan Claire, to be my wedded wife, to have and to hold from this day forward, for better, for worse, for richer, for poorer, for fairer or fouler, in sickness and in health, to love and to cherish, till death us depart, according to God's holy ordinance; and thereunto I plight thee my troth.'

'And now you, Megan Claire.'

'I, Megan Claire, take thee, John Clive, to be my wedded husband, to have and to hold from this day forward, for better, for worse, for richer, for poorer, for fairer or fouler, in sickness and in health, to love and to cherish, till death us depart, according to God's holy ordinance; and thereunto I plight thee my troth.'

'Who holds the bands that symbolise this union?'

Much stepped forward and handed Tuck the two matching rings. Tuck took them and placed each on Meg and John's fourth fingers of their left hands.

'Then I now pronounce you man and wife! You may k—'

The newlyweds didn't wait for permission and Tuck blushed, signing a cross in the air. The congregation erupted in cheers and whoops as Nasir and Will parted the kissing couple, lifting Meg Little up into the air and outside to the feast that the villagers had prepared. John followed, everyone shaking his hands and slapping him on the back.

'Congratulations, John!' Robin said as everyone started eating and the mead started flowing.

'To the bravest couple in Wickham, Sherwood, and beyond!' toasted Marion. 'Through hardships and strife we got them back together safe!'

'Thank you!' Meg replied, 'although "Lady Gisburne" did have a certain flair to it.'

Her deadpan expression cracked into a laugh and John laughed with her.

He had never been so happy. She was his true love, and he hers. And nothing could keep that from fading.

As the revelry continued into dusk, the noise suddenly descended into a hush. A few of the villagers gasped as they saw the imposing figure which stood at the edge of the village, its antlers curling high over its head.

'Herne!' John exclaimed.

'Children of Sherwood,' Herne said, his voice everywhere and nowhere. 'Children of Wickham.'

All in the congregation dropped to their knees.

'John Little… Meg Little… take the love that you have and keep it close. I, Herne the Hunter, Lord of the Trees, command it.

'The union here today is the union of us all. Together all, together none. You are blessed, each and every one of you. From this day forwards you should hold no fear. Even when the Apocalypse is upon us.'

There was no crack of lightning, no shimmering mist. Herne simply faded away, a spectral image imprinted on the minds of those before him.

Robin seemed unnerved and Marion sensed it.

'What's wrong?' she asked him, holding his arm.

'Oh, nothing, nothing,' he replied, pushing his frown aside to stand and raise a tankard with a smile. 'To Meg and John!'

'Meg and John!' the villagers replied as one, 'May they live happily ever after!'

Richard Carpenter's

ROBIN OF SHERWOOD

THE POWER OF THREE

Jennifer Ash

Richard Carpenter's

ROBIN OF SHERWOOD

THE
RED LORD

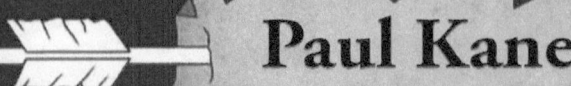

Paul Kane

www.ingramcontent.com/pod-product-compliance
Lightning Source LLC
Chambersburg PA
CBHW022041170626
46808CB00003B/1319